D0962161

## DO NOT REMOVE
## CARDS FROM POCKET

# THE MUSIC LOVERS

# JONATHAN VALIN

# THE MUSIC LOVERS

## A HARRY STONER NOVEL

**Delacorte Press**

Published by
Delacorte Press
Bantam Doubleday Dell Publishing Group, Inc.
666 Fifth Avenue
New York, New York 10103

Library of Congress Cataloging in Publication Data

Valin, Jonathan.
     The music lovers : a Harry Stoner mystery /
Jonathan Valin.
     p.  cm.
     ISBN 0-385-29965-6 : $19.95
     I. Title.
PS3572.A4125M87   1993
813'.54—dc20                        92-31323   CIP

Manufactured in the United States of America
Published simultaneously in Canada

April 1993

10  9  8  7  6  5  4  3  2  1

BVG

To Katherine,
as always,
and the Music Lovers everywhere

**HOW IT HAPPENED** I was in the office that Friday night, when I should have been in a bar like Arnold's eating a hot turkey sandwich and downing a cold beer, is in retrospect a piece of sobering irony: I'd stayed past my usual five-thirty closing to listen to music on the radio. WGUC was playing an opera by an obscure Polish composer named Szymanowski. I couldn't understand a word of the libretto, but I liked the choruses. I'm a sucker for the cracked harmonies of Middle European choirs with their sudden Slavic growls and weird, hilarious wails, like wind in organ pipes or criers in a minaret.

I probably would have stayed late even if Szymanowski hadn't caught my fancy. Business had been miserably slow all month and my lady friend, Jo Riley, was out of town for two weeks. I had nothing to do and nowhere to go. I consoled myself with the fact that it was

1

bitterly cold outside—the heart of January, with an Alberta Clipper sailing straight down the Ohio Valley. I had a bottle of Scotch in the desk drawer and a dime novel in the corncrib—a detective story written by some woman from Nome who was as arty as . . . well, as Szymanowski. The Scotch helped. It's amazing what Scotch will do for bad prose and Polish music.

Anyway the wind was whistling through the ranks of Szymanowski's chorus and the Nome detective was just working her way out of a "well of dreams"—close quarters, I guess, and damp as a diaper—when I heard the office door creak. It was either the door or a Polish tenor. I looked up and saw a shadow on the glass insert. It was too late to do anything about the bottle, but I chucked the paperback in a wastebasket and took my feet off the desk just as a bent man in a nylon jacket and a knit cap stepped into the room. He was carrying a record jacket in his right hand. His left hand and forearm were wrapped in a soft cast.

He swiped the cap off his head and folded it up carefully before tucking it in his jacket pocket like a linen hankie.

"I'm always leaving these things behind," he explained in a squeaky voice. "Hats, gloves, scarves, umbrellas. My honey, Sheila, says I'd lose my head if it weren't screwed on."

The man walked over to my desk.

He was one of the S-shaped people, hunched at the shoulder, caved at the chest, a little paunchy around the middle, and no ass at all. In fact his pants, chinos with a dark muddy stain on one cuff, began to slip down his legs as soon as he stepped through the door. By the time he got to the chair they were halfway off his butt. He put the record on the desk and hiked the chinos up with his good hand, tucking his lumberjack shirt in at the back.

"You have no idea what it's like going through life with your ass hanging out," he said as he sat down on the chair.

"It must be humbling."

"Humbling is the word."

He was a short man in his mid-forties, with lanky brown hair going gray at the temples and a Charlie Chaplin mustache the color of tobacco ash beneath a long, thin nose. He wore sixties-style, wire-rimmed specs with lenses so thick his watery blue eyes seemed to pop from his face.

The odd little man took in my barren office as I took him in. Although he wasn't dilapidated enough to be homeless, he had the markings of a lost soul—one of the sixties' remnant who never crossed the divide of the Reagan years into the kinder, gentler polity of the nineties. He'd have no money, of course, or next to none. Which meant he'd be a charity case, which meant I couldn't afford him. Not in that kinder, gentler year.

I'd already decided to show him the gate when he said something that changed my mind.

Still staring thoughtfully into space he raised his good hand and dropped it in a downbeat timed to the music that was playing on the radio. He turned to me with a pleasant smile.

"That's Szymanowski, isn't it? *King Roger?*"

Anyone who knew that was worth hearing out.

The odd little man with the pop-eyes and tooth-brush mustache had a musician's name, Leon Tubin.

"Like the Estonian composer," he said. "Do you know Tubin's violin concerto?"

I shook my head. "I didn't know Szymanowski either until this afternoon. You did, though."

Leon Tubin shrugged his round shoulders. "It's a gift I have. I can barely remember my own phone number. I'm at sea in a grocery store without a shopping list. I don't dare park in a lot that has more than two aisles. But I can usually tell you who composed a piece of classical music after hearing a bar or two."

"You must do a lot of listening," I said, eyeing the record he'd carried in with him and dropped on the desk. Although I was looking at it upside-down, it appeared to be a photograph of dancing legs and a flouncy skirt.

"Classical music is my great love," he said. "Not counting Sheila, of course. I compose music, too."

"For a living?"

"For a living, if one can call it that, I'm a part-time instructor at NKSU. I teach introductory math—you know, calc and algebra? I also teach night school on Tuesdays and Thursdays."

"That doesn't leave a lot of time for composition."

The little man sighed. "Don't I know it. I'm a week-end musician—that's what Strauss called Mahler. Not that I'm another Mahler. But on a good Sunday afternoon I half-believe I have something worthwhile to say."

4

"What happened to your hand?" I asked.

Leon Tubin stared bitterly at the soft cast on his left arm. "That's what I came to talk to you about. That and the record, of course."

He pushed the album jacket across the desk.

I swiveled it around and picked it up. It was a recording of Offenbach's *Gaîté Parisienne,* conducted by Arthur Fiedler. The cover did, indeed, picture dancing legs and a flouncy skirt—a chorine doing the can-can. There was no record inside the jacket.

"That is—or was before it was stolen from me— RCA number 1817," Leon Tubin said. "One of the very first stereo recordings."

"Was it valuable?"

"Quite valuable from a collector's standpoint. The music itself isn't to my taste."

"I thought these things were being replaced," I said, pitching the empty jacket back on the desk. "You know, CD's and all."

Leon Tubin started as if I'd cursed God in French.

"CD's are shit," he said with sudden, surprising bitterness. "Horrible, emasculated travesties of their analog originals. They are nothing more than a plot concocted by greedy record companies to gull brainless consumers into discarding their vinyl and repurchasing the very same performances in overpriced, sonically inferior forms. It makes me furious to think that a medium which has preserved some of the greatest performances of the greatest music ever written is being sacrificed wholly for gain. These things are priceless time machines." He tapped the album with his forefinger. "What you're listening to on an analog disc is an exact replica of a unique moment in history. When you play this record, for instance, you're hearing music being born on a summer afternoon in 1954—the actual waves of sound created by the Boston Pops, echoing through Symphony Hall and striking the microphones' diaphragms. It's life itself you're listening to. Not a series of digits."

He leaned back in his chair, bright-eyed and invigorated by his oration. I could tell from the look on his face that he could ride this particular hobbyhorse all night and into the morning—and fully expected me to hop on behind. I was interested in stereo but not enough to engage in a trail ride with a veteran bore.

"Getting back to your arm."

Leon Tubin allowed himself a moment's disappointment when I didn't saddle up.

"My arm was broken by a thief," he said, a touch sullenly. "This man—a man whose name I know—sneaked into my home and stole thirty-five of my most valuable records."

"Did you call the police?" I asked.

"Of course. Insufficient evidence, *they* said. I say if it looks like a duck and walks like a duck, it's a duck."

"Who is this duck?"

"Sherwood Loeffler is the bastard's name."

"And what would you have me do with this Sherwood Loeffler?"

Leon Tubin drew himself up in the chair. "I would like to hire you to kill him."

"Uh-huh."

"Of course I know that isn't possible." But a note of hope persisted in his voice like a pedal point.

"It is not possible," I said flatly. "At least, it's not possible at this window."

"Short of that, I would like you to recover my records and to prove that Sherwood Loeffler is the culprit." He gave me a slightly withering look. "Is *that* possible?"

"For a fee, yes."

"Ah, your fee."

Leon Tubin reached into his pants pocket and pulled out one of the largest wads of paper money I'd seen this side of a Monopoly game. I actually had to look at the bills twice—to make sure they didn't have pictures of Mr. Moneybags on them.

"You make that kind of dough teaching math, Leon?"

The little man smiled. "Hardly. In my spare time I sell records, Mr. Stoner. Vinyl, analog records." He separated each word for emphasis. "The thirty-five that were stolen from me are worth roughly ten thousand dollars in today's market, considerably more in New York or Tokyo."

"Christ," I said, "they're like grams of cocaine."

"Better," Leon Tubin said. "They make music and they're legal."

# 2

**OF COURSE, I TOOK THE CASE.** I'd been living off my Visa card and Jo's Christmas bonus since New Year's Day. The five-hundred-dollar retainer that Leon Tubin gave me—in crisp new hundreds no less—was the most cash I'd seen in three weeks. So what if he was a little odd? I can work odd, I told myself.

Off we went to Leon Tubin's house—my little Pinto making its way through the bright and frosty snow. I nearly slid into an embankment at the Elberon overpass. Aside from that the trip down River Road to Saylor Park was uneventful.

Along the way Leon filled me in on the used record business. Used vinyl, analog records. I heard all about RCA's, EMI's, London Bluebacks, Lyritas, English Deccas, and the best of the best, Mercury Living Presences. I discovered that the finest RCA Victor recordings had a dog pictured on their label—a little dog who listens to his dead master's voice on a windup phonograph. But it wasn't just any little dog—on the finest RCA's the dog was "shaded."

"Shaded, like half in light, half in shade?"

"No," Leon said. "The shaded area surrounds the little dog like a dark backdrop."

"What about the Mercuries? Do they have dogs on them, too?"

"No. Just the words 'Mercury Stereo' on top of the label, and 'Living Presence—High Fidelity' on the bottom along with a line drawing of Mercury in his winged hat."

"What makes these records so special?"

Leon Tubin shut his eyes as if in silent prayer. "The sound, man. The sound."

Leon's house was just a block north of River Road in the old, riverside community of Saylor Park. It was a small, tidy-looking bungalow—white stucco with a pitched roof and a walled-in porch. The rest of the street was lined with the same foursquare homes—some of them still decked with Christmas lights.

We parked in Leon's driveway, in front of a basement garage, and walked up a short flight of steps to the front door. Someone had salted the stairs to melt the snow, and the rock salt crunched like plastic popcorn underfoot. When we got to the door Leon held a hand to my chest.

"Would you mind waiting outside for a second, Harry," he said. "I wanta make sure that Sheila is decent."

He slid a key in the lock, opened the door, and

went in. A moment or two later he came back out with a glum look on his face.

"She's kinda in a bad mood," he said.

"You want me to come back?"

He thought about it for a second. "No. The sooner you get going on this, the sooner that bastard will be behind bars."

He opened the door and I stepped into Leon Tubin's living room. There was a couch with a throw to the right, a portal leading to a dark dining room at the rear, and on the left the largest pair of stereo speakers I'd ever seen. At least I thought they were speakers—they looked like screen doors with hardwood frames and had wires the size of garden hoses running from somewhere behind them over to a bank of glowing boxes.

"They're electrostatic," Leon said.

"Every bit of it," I said, looking them over. "These things make music?"

"Wonderfully. I could fire them up, if you like."

"Maybe we should look at the records first."

"You've ruined his day," a woman called out.

I looked up and saw a fortyish blonde dressed in a man's white dress shirt and a black leotard, standing in the dining room portal. She had a pair of half-frame glasses perched on her forehead, a cigarette in her lips, and a glass of whiskey in her right hand. She held a paperback novel in her left hand—the same damn book I'd been reading at the office. The detective story about the well of dreams.

"I'm Sheila Mozkowski," she said, putting the book

down on a cane table and holding out her hand to shake. "Leon's moll."

She smiled a pretty smile and shook with me, holding my hand a beat or so longer than felt right.

"Give the man his hand back, Sheila," Leon said, forcing a smile.

"Oh, for chrissake." She dropped my hand. "So you're the detective?"

"That's me."

"Very nice," she said, looking me up and down. "Especially since we picked you out of the phone book more or less at random. Loved the big eye in your ad."

"It's supposed to be a joke—you know, private eye?"

"Ha-ha," the woman said distinctly. "You a sixties guy, Harry? You look like a sixties guy."

I nodded. "Sixties to the bone."

"That's the way we are—Leon and me. Leftovers in the refrigerator of life." She laughed, showing a set of large white teeth.

She was a brazen thing and damn good-looking. A little wrinkled by her years in the fridge, but well preserved, with eyes the color of hothouse grapes and a build like the hothouse itself. She certainly made an odd accompanist to Leon Tubin, the music lover. But the case had started in the key of odd.

"Pull up a chair and Leon'll break out some o.z. and crank up the system. I've had a hard day and I feel like some music."

She sat down on the couch and patted the cushion beside her.

"C'mon. Sit down, for chrissake. Tell me your sign

and who you've been screwing. Oops, I almost said the F-word." She looked up at Leon, who was staring at her with a pasty grin. "I'm sorry, honey, I know that's just for you—like mother's milk."

"You're being rude to our guest, Sheila," Leon said, trying to keep his voice level and not succeeding.

"Who the hell asked me whether I wanted to entertain a guest?"

"You know we discussed this."

"*You* discussed it," the woman said sharply. "And I am sick to death of hearing you carry on like a child over a bunch of goddamn records you paid a buck apiece for. I mean why can't you just forget about it. You'll get more of them—you know it and so do I. Why do you have to make a federal case out of it, if you get my drift?"

I assumed she was talking about me—and my eye.

"It's the principle of the thing."

"Right. Are we going to listen to music or what?" she said directly to me.

"I think I'll have to pass."

Looking disgusted, Sheila Mozkowski picked up a remote control and flipped on a TV like she was flipping Leon and me off. She stared at the screen and sipped her drink as if we'd already left the room.

"C'mon, Harry," Leon said in a tiny voice. "The records are downstairs in the basement."

Leon led me through a dark dining room into a small white kitchen, then down a flight of stairs to the basement.

"I'm sorry about Sheila," he said.

"Don't worry about it."

"She just hasn't been the same since the records were stolen," he said with a sigh. "Or maybe I haven't been the same."

"How long have you two been together?" I asked.

"Thirteen years, if you can believe it. We met in a bookstore in Anaheim where Sheila clerked and . . . just hit it off. We both liked the same things—music and books. She's a classically trained singer, you know. Well, of course you didn't know that. But she is. She can sing anything. Anything. And she plays the piano, too. She's so talented. I honestly don't know what she sees in me."

Leon dropped his head and stared forlornly at the floor.

"Let's look at the records," I said.

"Of course," the little man said.

Leon made his way through the dark room to a wall switch and flipped it on. Paneled fluorescents went on overhead, lighting up the entire basement. I blinked once and sucked in my breath. The walls were covered, every inch of them from floor to ceiling, with huge steel bookshelves filled with records. King-sized mosaics of records—their parti-colored spines making weird, swirling patterns against the stippled plaster of the walls.

"Jesus Christ," I said with genuine awe. "How many records do you own?"

"Twenty-three thousand, eight hundred and fifty-two," he said with pride. "My ambition is to own them all."

"Every record?"

"I have a ways to go, yet," he said.

I walked over to a shelf and ran a finger along the

spines of the jackets. "How the hell did you figure out that any of them were missing?"

"Oh, I have an elaborate cataloging system." Leon patted the strut of one of the bookcases. "I was a library sciences major in college. And I learned how to sort and catalog just about anything. It's one of those skills that have limited applications outside the library profession. Since I didn't become a librarian I've only been able to make use of it a few times in my life—the records being one of them. I have them arranged in numerical order by label. I also have separate catalog of titles, composers, and artists. I'm nothing if not thorough."

"You'd make a good accountant."

Leon flushed. "What an odd thing to say."

"Where'd the records come from?" I asked.

"I bought a large number of them in college. It was practically all I ever spent money on—records and a few books, and once Sheila talked me into buying a car. The rest I've acquired over the last thirteen years at yard sales, estate sales, library sales, thrift shops, used record stores. You name a hole in the wall and I've looked in it."

Leon walked across the room to a bookcase standing beside what I took to be the door leading to the garage. "This, as they say, is the scene of the crime."

He pointed to a shelf at eye height. Unlike every other shelf in the room it was not fully packed with records. There were several conspicuously empty slots.

"I kept the cream of my collection on this shelf."

I looked it over. There were spots of dried detergent on the metal shaped like a washerwoman's tears.

"Has someone wiped this shelf off since the records were stolen?"

"Yeah, probably. Sheila's been down here, I think. Heck, I might have done it myself. Sherwood wouldn't be stupid enough to leave fingerprints, anyway."

"What makes you so certain that this guy, Sherwood, did it?"

"Because he told me he was going to do it," Leon said.

"He *told* you."

"In so many words."

I gave the little man a long look. "Exactly how many words is that, Leon? You're making a serious accusation that could land someone in jail. If the records are worth what you say they are this is felony–grand theft."

"You think I don't know how serious this is?" he said indignantly. "My *Hi-Fi Espagnol* was worth fifteen hundred bucks. My *Royal Ballet Gala* two grand. My Reiner *Thus Sprake* close to eight. Sherwood Loeffler knew that I kept those records—and many others just as valuable—on this shelf. He also knew I was going to the symphony last Friday night—a performance that he did not attend and he attends the CSO concerts religiously." Leon stuck out his hand and began peeling back his fingers. "Means, motive, opportunity."

"Sort of," I said with a smile. "This Loeffler is a friend of yours?"

"An acquaintance. A group of us get together to listen to music each week. He is part of the group."

"How long has this group of yours been meeting?"

"Ten years," Leon Tubin said.

I started to smile. "Loeffler has been coming to your house for ten years. And you say he's just an acquaintance?"

"All right, he's more than an acquaintance," Leon said, reddening. "Ninety percent of violent crimes occur between people who know each other."

"You keep stats?"

"I'm just saying it's not uncommon for . . . friends to commit crimes against friends."

"Why did he wait ten years to do it?"

Leon sighed. "We had a fight. Two weeks ago, Wednesday. We'd gone to a library record sale at the downtown branch, and we had a fight over a record I found in one of the dollar bins."

"Loeffler's a collector, too?"

"Yes," Leon said grudgingly. "Although all he really cares about is the sound of the records—not the music itself."

"What record did you boys fight over?"

"RCA LSC-1817, the Offenbach *Gaîté* I brought to your office."

"I take it that was quite a find?"

Leon nodded. "It's the jackpot—or almost. Five hundred bucks, give or take a hundred. I could scarcely believe it was sitting there in one of the charity donation bins. Of course, Sherwood claimed that he'd spotted it first. Which was a lie. And when I refused to hand it over to him he made a ruckus right there on the ground floor of the library—shouting at me, calling me names. He never comes right out and calls me a kike or a sheeny—at least not to my face. But you know that's what he's thinking. It's amazing the depths a civilized man can sink to when he doesn't get a shaded dog."

Leon tsk'd with his lips, while I bit mine.

"Two days later, a week ago last Friday, we had our weekly meeting, which just happened to be scheduled for my house. We went down to the basement to pick out the records for the evening's listening session—each of us picks a record. I chose LSC-1817, of course, my new acquisition. Which was probably a mistake. Sherwood thought I was rubbing it in."

"Were you?"

"A little bit," Leon admitted. "After the way he'd behaved he deserved it. Anyway he started up again, talking about how he just got done reading Nietzsche, which is always his prelude to a little sly anti-Semitism. You know, the Jews having a slave mentality, how they're incapable of original thought. He loves to trot out the anti-Semitic passages in Nietzsche and Heidegger to get my goat. He especially likes to quote Jews who denigrate Jews, like Wittgenstein and Marx do. It goes without saying that Wagner is his favorite composer—he seems to be the perennial favorite of white, Anglo-Saxon failures. Did you know that Wagner was less than five feet tall? The pianist Anton Rubinstein used to carry him around in his arms like a puppet. The Nazi's darling was a Nibelung. Hell, I let him rant and went back upstairs. But he wouldn't leave it alone. Late that evening he made the threat."

"What threat?"

Leon drew himself up on his toes and dropped his voice an octave—presumably aping his rival. "He said,

'You cheated me out of that record, you little nerd. And I'm going to get it back.'

" 'Over my dead body,' I told him.

" 'It can be arranged,' he said with a malicious smile. 'One way or another that record is going to be mine. Consider this your last warning.' "

Leon fetched a long sigh. "I didn't take him seriously. Who's gonna take a *meshuggy* like that seriously? I guess I should have, though, the way things worked out. After the records were stolen I confronted him in his office. That's when the incident with my arm occurred."

"He broke your arm?"

"Not exactly." Leon turned his head to avoid looking me in the eye. "I got a little hot under the collar and accused him of stealing my records. Sherwood just laughed and called me a little nerd again. So I took a swipe at him, missed, and . . . hit the wall."

"And broke your arm."

He nodded.

I stared at Leon Tubin. "You *really* think this guy took your records, Leon? Or are you just mad about being called names and breaking your arm?"

"He took them, Harry," Leon said, raising his head with a doleful look. "Or he hired somebody to do it. I know he did. You see, a record is worth considerably less without its jacket. The thief took both the records and the jackets of the other thirty-four records he stole. But he left the jacket of LSC-1817 on the floor—just to let me know who was behind the theft. That's the way Sherwood Loeffler's evil, bigoted mind works."

"All right," I said. "Where can I find him?"

"He lives in Walnut Hills. On Fairfield Avenue. You

can catch him there most evenings and weekends, or at work during the weekdays."

"Where is work?"

"At NKSU," Leon Tubin said. "He's a part-time instructor in the Classics Department."

**3**

**IN MY EXPERIENCE** classics instructors—even small-minded, bigoted, part-time classics instructors—rarely break into homes to steal records.

There was no point in telling Leon this. He was past listening to reason. He'd paid me five hundred dollars to make Loeffler squirm, and he expected to see some squirming. Since there was no way around it I told Leon I'd visit his nemesis the following afternoon. But I had the feeling that Loeffler wasn't going to get me any closer to the stolen records, and having accepted Leon's retainer I felt obliged to find the damn things in spite of his obsession.

I decided to work around Loeffler, but delicately so Leon still felt like he was getting his groat's worth of vengeance. When I brought the fingerprint kit in from the trunk of the car I told him it was because an amateur thief like Loeffler might well have left some telltale prints without realizing it.

"He's smart, Harry," Leon said, shaking his head. "He probably wore gloves. Or his lackey did."

"I'll use cyanoacrylate," I said in my best cryptic detective's manner. I could almost feel my eyes slanting and a number-one son sprouting from my forehead.

Anyway Leon seemed to buy it. Which bought me a half-hour's *potchkying* around the basement, dusting the shelf and the door. I didn't really expect to find anything that the cops hadn't already found, especially since the shelf had been wiped clean. But there was an off-chance that the I.O.'s hadn't dusted for prints and that the two or three latents I did manage to lift could be tagged by the CPD.

After packing up the kit I sat down with Leon at a little folding table near the washing machine and went through the details of the robbery. The thief had to have gotten into the house somehow, and the garage door seemed like the best avenue of entry and escape, since it was closest to the records and easiest to jimmy. I started off by asking Leon whether he'd locked the garage and the basement doors before leaving for the concert on Friday night.

"I'm not sure they were locked," Leon said, casting a dark look through the ceiling at his girlfriend. "Sheila pulled the car out while I was inside the house. We were in a rush so I didn't check to make sure she'd locked up. God knows I've told her enough times to keep the garage and basement doors locked. But I didn't check."

"Were they locked when you got home?"

"Yes. Both of them."

"And the front door?"

"That I'm sure I locked. After I discovered the theft I examined it carefully. So did the police. They found no signs of—how did they put it—forced entry." Leon smiled. "Sheila told them they were looking at the wrong opening."

I laughed.

"The cops seemed to think that the thief *did* get in through the unlocked garage and basement doors—locking them behind him on the way out."

"Or he might have had a key," I said.

Leon shook his head. "The cops said that, too. Only no one has a key, except for Sheila and me. Harry, we were only gone three or four hours. Whoever Sherwood hired to do this thing obviously knew we'd be out. It was just his good luck—and my bad—that he found both doors unlocked. Otherwise I'm sure he would have broken in some other way."

"For the sake of argument let's pretend that Sherwood Loeffler isn't the only possible suspect."

Leon started to fidget but I held up a hand.

"Work with me on this, Leon."

"All right," he said grudgingly, "but you're sounding more and more like the cops."

There's a coincidence, I said to myself. To Leon, I said, "Who else knew that you kept valuable records on that one shelf?"

"The guys in the club, of course."

I took out my official detective's notebook and pencil. "And they would be?"

"Pavel Fleischer, Larry Peacock, Hank Diamond, Dave Barber. Oh, and LeRoy Anderson."

"Isn't he a composer, too?"

Leon smiled. "This LeRoy Anderson is a building contractor. He's also one of my oldest friends."

"You have addresses for these guys?" I asked.

"Sure. But there's no point in getting any of them involved. I *know* who did this, Harry."

"Bear with me, Leon. Did your neighbors see anyone come in or go out of your house while you and Sheila were at the concert?"

Leon shook his head. "The Jaspers were in L.A., visiting family. And the Wemblows went to the same concert we went to. In fact I ran into Hal at Music Hall during the first intermission."

"We have no witnesses, then," I said, flipping the official notebook shut and tucking it and the official pencil back in my jacket.

"No witnesses."

"All right, we'll try a different tack. Whoever stole the records had to know which ones were valuable, right?"

"Of course. He only took the most expensive ones."

"If—if, mind you—he didn't steal the records for his own collection, where would he go to fence them?"

"Beg pardon?" Leon said.

"Who would buy them from him?"

Leon shrugged. "Practically any knowledgeable collector of vinyl would, as well as many dealers here in town. Of course, if he was after top dollar he would either try to sell them on his own through the mail or to a dealer in New York, L.A., San Francisco, or Tokyo. Selling them locally he'd only get a third or fourth of their potential value."

"So we're dealing with a highly specialized thief," I said, with the sinking feeling that I was painting myself into the same corner Leon was standing in. "This is a guy who knows records and the record-selling business. Or he is working for someone else who knows about them. Or he is a collector himself."

"Like I've been saying all along, it was Sherwood Loeffler," Leon Tubin said conclusively.

"Maybe," I said, although I didn't believe it.

=====

I ended up taking Leon's and Sheila's fingerprints before I left—to compare with the three that I'd lifted from the basement. The girlfriend made another scene when I'd finished. Although Leon had claimed they were soulmates I certainly didn't get that impression. Sheila Mozkowski seemed a good deal coarser and tougher than Leon Tubin—and a lot more experienced in the ways of the world. She had obviously been with other men before she ended up with Leon—and I would have bet that the least of them could have eaten the little man for breakfast. Of course that difference in itself might have been explained the attraction—at least on her side.

On Leon's side the attraction was plain. She was a beautiful woman who had somehow fallen to earth in his backyard, and he worshipped her in the doomed, touching way that ugly men worship beautiful women. As a corollary to that worship he was willing to shut an eye—or maybe two—whenever she strayed. And as it turned out he'd had to shut one that night.

The trouble started when Leon insisted that I listen

to his stereo before leaving. I'd been around stereophiles before—flirted with the obsession myself—so I knew how badly he wanted to show his system off. I honestly thought that part of the reason he'd paid me five hundred bucks was to get me over to his house to listen to his rig.

Anyway, I said yes and sat down on the couch beside Sheila, who was definitely three sheets to the wind at that point. Almost immediately Leon started fiddling with the equipment and at the same time directing me around the couch like a portrait photographer.

"You've gotta sit a little to the left, Harry," he said, waving one hand savagely and tilting his screen doors with the other. "More to the left. These things are electrostats and they beam like crazy. You gotta be right in the middle if it's gonna sound real."

The result of his direction was that I practically ended up in Sheila Mozkowski's lap.

"Cozy, huh," she said, running a finger up my arm. "How 'bout turning off the lights, Leon. It's better in the dark."

"She's right," Leon said with an agreeable smile. "The speakers just disappear in the dark—like you're in a concert hall."

"I'll close my eyes and use my imagination."

"Whatever."

Leon ducked behind one of the speakers and went back to work, moving the things an inch or two to the right or left, tilting them, pivoting them, lifting them and redepositing them in a slightly different spot. He got so red-faced and sweaty I thought he might pass out.

"You want a hand with those?" I asked him, as he struggled one last time with his gigantic obsessions.

"*You* have nice hands," Sheila Mozkowski said, playing suggestively with my fingers.

I couldn't ignore her—that would have been dangerous. So I picked her hand up off mine and put it gently back in her lap.

"You're no fun at all," the woman said with an abrupt laugh. "You aren't queer, are you?"

"As a three-dollar bill."

"No, you're not. I'm just drunk and coming on too strong. And you're playing hard to get. It's O.K. Wanna hear a joke?"

"Sure, why not?"

"How does a kid know when his sister has her period?"

"I give up."

"When Daddy's dick tastes bad."

Sheila Mozkowski started to laugh so hard she spilled the glass of whiskey on her leotard.

"Some joke, huh?" she said, wiping the booze off with her free hand. "I read it in a book called *London Fields*. A psychopath says it to somebody in a bar. I forget who."

"It's a great little ice-breaker."

"I think it's the ugliest joke I've ever heard," she said flatly.

"Sheila," Leon called out from behind the speaker. "Leave the man alone, will you?"

"Shut the hell up, Leon. Go diddle your stereo. You and your friend diddle your friggin' stereo. Sheila's going to bed."

The woman got unsteadily to her feet.

"Don't you want to hear some music?" Leon called out.

"Christ," the woman said miserably.

Wobbling, she wandered out of the room.

A few seconds later Leon came out from behind the speakers. I thought he'd been hiding there until she left. There was no question that he'd overheard all that had gone on between Sheila and me. She'd wanted him to hear it. Maybe he'd wanted to listen.

"Sometimes I'd like to slap her," he said, choking on a smile. "Just . . . slap her."

I didn't say anything. What could I say?

"I love her so much, goddamnit. And she just keeps doing this terrible, embarrassing stuff." He swallowed hard. "She's not always this way, believe me. It's just been the weeks since the break-in. She's been so tense and when she drinks . . ."

I thought perhaps the scene with Sheila had killed his interest in stereo. But I think it would have taken a bullet in the brain to do that.

Collecting himself he walked over to the turntable and dropped the stylus on a record. A piano started to play a Schoenberg piece. And for a second I thought that Sheila had sat down to a Steinway somewhere in that dark house and begun to perform.

"Is that Sheila playing the piano?" I asked.

When I looked up at Leon Tubin he was smiling again—this time for real.

"You don't know how good you just made me feel."

▬▬▬▬

On the way back to town I thought a little better of Sheila Mozkowski. Day after day of the kind of fiddling I'd witnessed—finical, exasperating, exacting fiddling— might have taken the bloom off the rose for me, too. And yet the odd little man had performed an undeni- able feat of magic at the end of that lousy night: he'd made a piano appear in his living room.

I made myself appear in a bar before turning for home—Arnold's on East Eighth Street—where I found a dark corner in which to sulk and drink. I missed Jo. I missed the steady work that kept me from taking on sad cases like Leon and Sheila. And I missed the good old days, those black vinyl days before Reagan and Bush and the young Republicans I used to laugh at in college somehow took over the country and slammed the refrig- erator door shut on me and Leon and Sheila Mozkow- ski. I wondered if I looked as burned-out to them as they had looked to me: Leon with his throwback hobby, and Sheila with her bottle and (presumably) her back- door men. That's what my generation had come to: the minimal, secondhand passions of middle age. And we were going to change the world.

About the third Scotch it came to me that the refrig- erator light doesn't stay on once that door is shut. It also came to me that I was going to have to confront Sher- wood Loeffler in the morning with Leon's preposterous charge. It was enough to make me order another drink and pay for it with one of Leon Tubin's crisp new hun- dred-dollar bills.

# 4

SHERWOOD LOEFFLER lived in a big old house near the corner of Fairfield and Madison roads in East Walnut Hills. With its roof covered by the light snow that had fallen early that Saturday morning it was Currier & Ives Americana: a rambling yellow frame colonial, with cupolas and dormers and a curving veranda that swept around the corners at each end.

It was past noon when I pulled up in front of it. I'd already spent half the morning avoiding the place. I'd managed to kill an early hour conning a lab technician at the CPD into running the prints I'd lifted from Leon's basement, and another wheedling Al Foster, my friend in homicide, into throwing a little marshal work my way—warrants, bail skips, anything that would make me a kinder, gentler, less disturbing buck. The way I was looking at it, there wasn't going to be much future in the Leon Tubin case—once I got past the exquisite embarrassment of interviewing Loeffler.

According to Al the robbery division had already put Leon's records on the stolen goods hot sheet—serial numbers, pressing numbers, shaded dogs, Mercury hats, and all. And that meant that pawnshops, junk shops, used record stores, independent dealers, even stereo equipment salesmen would automatically be notified about the theft. Which left me very little to do.

Before leaving Leon's house the previous night I'd managed to get the phone numbers and addresses of the other members of his stereo club. I'd even called a few after finishing with Al—more foot-dragging before the confrontation with Loeffler. The only one I'd found at home was the building contractor LeRoy Anderson, who turned out to be retired. He'd already heard about the burglary through the stereo grapevine and was willing to talk to me. I told the guy I'd call him back later in the day, figuring that if worse came to worst I could use him as penance for the five-hundred-dollar retainer, although Sherwood Loeffler seemed like penance enough.

After getting off the phone with Anderson I'd bought myself lunch at Izzy's (killing another thirty minutes) and stopped back at the office (fifteen), hoping there'd be honest, compelling work on the answering machine. But there was no work, and there was no way around Sherwood Loeffler.

I stared at his house for a long time before getting up the nerve to step out into the cold. A child's snow-covered, blue plastic tricycle was sitting beside the walk which led to the front door. The very sight of it made me cringe. The guy had kids. A picture-book house. A job at a university.

Somehow I kept walking up to the door. A wilted brown holly wreath, left over from Christmas, surrounded the brass knocker. Behind the door I could hear the gabble of children's voices, the thud of footsteps on a staircase, and faintly, but unmistakably, the sound of Valkyries riding the night wind. Leon had told me Sherwood Loeffler was a Wagnerian. But he hadn't told me the half of it.

I raised the brass knocker and let it drop. A moment later a huge man answered. He had a long, pale, pugnacious face capped on top with flaming red hair streaked with gray and on bottom with a stiff conical beard that jutted straight out from his chin like a miss with an ice cream cone.

I'm six feet three, two hundred pounds. But this guy dwarfed me. He was six eight if he was an inch, maybe two hundred and sixty pounds. And he had a voice that fit his size—a booming bass-baritone that, with the Valkyries "Heihoing" in the background, made me think of the giants Fafner and Fasolt.

"What kin I do for you?" the huge man bellowed, tilting his head back and pointing that beard at me like a loaded ice cream cone.

There was a bit of Appalachia in his voice, West Virginia or eastern Kentucky.

"Are you Sherwood Loeffler?"

"I am," he said, drawing himself up another imposing inch or so. I wondered how much more spare height he had hidden on his body.

A couple of wide-eyed kids had wandered in from

somewhere else in the house—pretty little five- or six-year-old girls. They huddled around their father's legs, like the urchins in Father Christmas's robes.

"My name is Stoner, Mr. Loeffler." I handed him a card. "If you've got a minute I'd like to ask you a few questions."

Sherwood Loeffler looked down at the two little girls, who were staring up at him as if he were perched in a tree.

"Scat," he boomed.

They giggled and ran off.

Loeffler pulled a pair of reading glasses from his pocket and stuck them on his nose, pinning them to his face with a forefinger.

He scanned the card and began to laugh—a big, chiming laugh like a carillon going off in a church steeple.

"You're working for Leon, ain't you? The nerd went and hired him a detective." Stepping back from the door, he waved me through with a sweep of one massive arm. "Come in. Come in, for chrissake. This is gonna be amusing."

═══════

We went into what Sherwood Loeffler called his "sitting room." A sprung armchair and a Tuxedo sofa that looked like it had spent most of its life in a hotel lobby were sitting on one wall, and a pair of stereo speakers—squat little numbers shaped like radiators—on the other. A portal on the left led to an anteroom.

The house was in less good repair than I'd thought from the outside. Several of the sitting room walls had unpainted patches of plaster on them and there was a blistering water stain on the ceiling. When I thought about it, it stood to reason that the house would be in disrepair—Loeffler was an instructor, making the same kind of money that Leon made. He'd probably gotten the place for a song, back in the days when yuppies armed with urban renewal loans were farming that rundown section of East Walnut Hills. But unlike the yuppies he'd never had the dough to restore the place—or even to keep it up.

Although the house was as outsized as the man himself—as large as Leon's had been small—I had a strong sense of déjà vu when I sat down on his Goodwill sofa and stared across the room at the two squat speakers.

"They're electrostats," Sherwood Loeffler said, and ran a proud hand delicately across the top of one of the radiators. "Much better than Leon's gaudy stuff."

"I'm sure they're great."

"Care to hear anything?" he said with some of the same barely contained excitement I'd seen on Leon's face—like a man trying not to come too soon.

The way to a stereophile's heart is through his system.

"Love to," I said. "Some Wagner, perhaps?"

The huge man's face lit up with joy.

"You're a Wagner-lover?"

"My favorite composer."

Sherwood Loeffler actually yipped with pleasure, rubbing his big hands together so vigorously he could have made sparks.

"Wha'd'ya want to hear, Harry. How 'bout *Meistersinger*?"

"*Meistersinger* would be great, Sherwood."

Instant pals.

Loeffler strode across the room, through the portal into the anteroom. Through the opening I could see several bookshelves filled with records.

A few second later the radiators in the sitting room started making music. The sound wasn't as massive and immediate as Leon's had been. But it was sweeter, fuller, and, in its own right, just as realistic.

Loeffler obviously had a heavy sense of humor, because he'd put on the singing contest between Walther von Stolzing and Sixtus Beckmesser. He came striding back into the room and sat down on a ratty chair beside the couch.

"You know Beckmesser was modeled on a Jewish music critic named Eduard Hanslick," Loeffler said—to point the irony. "It's the only reason Hanslick's remembered today. Because big, bad Richard Wagner immortalized him in song."

There was a needling playfulness in Loeffler's voice that was a bit alarming. I began to wonder if he really had bought my act, or if he'd seen through it and was using *Meistersinger* to teach me a lesson about music, Wagner, and Leon Tubin.

"This is Von Karajan's '51 mono. Those old Nazis sure could play. And this was their favorite piece. Kin you imagine that? Everybody thinks it was the Ring, but it was *Meistersinger*. *Meistersinger* and Bruckner. Hitler never would allow *Siegfried* or *Götterdämmerung* to be performed in his presence. Smacked too much of *das Ende,* I guess."

Now I was convinced he was toying with me. So I struck back, weakly.

"I guess you don't listen to them either."

The huge man drew himself up in the chair with a look of mock outrage. "Christ, no. I love them both. I love all great music. And my boy Richard's top of the heap. Why the whole twentieth century streams out of him like the headwaters of the Nile. Ya know Hans Richter, the conductor, called him Richard the First. Strauss was Richard the Third." Grinning, Loeffler said, "There wasn't any Second."

In the background Walther was singing his grand love song to win Eva. Loeffler shut his eyes and let his right hand lilt through the air, as if it were buoyed by the music itself.

"I guess Leon told you I stole his records, didn't he?" he said, eyes shut.

"He mentioned the possibility."

Loeffler chuckled to himself. "I bet he did. I've had the police here twice this week. A newspaper reporter. And now you, Harry. I think ol' Leon has sprung a serious leak."

"He claims you threatened him, Sherwood."

Sherwood Loeffler slowly opened his big, blue eyes and looked over at me with stunned innocence. "Shocking, ain't it? Just shocking that a man could make baseless accusations against another man solely out of jealous spite. Turn his household upside-down. Cause his reputation grievous harm. Why it's as bad as attacking somebody on the basis of their religion."

"Let's cut the crap, Sherwood."

"Glad to, Harry," he said, drawing himself up in the chair. "I didn't threaten Leon—just ask the other boys in the club. And I didn't steal a thing from that crybaby, either. On the contrary, he stole something quite valuable from me."

"You mean besides your reputation?"

Sherwood Loeffler laughed. "Naw, I wasn't referring to my reputation. I'm referring to LSC-1817. Offenbach's *Gaîté Parisienne*. That was my record, Harry. A mint, 10/S, shaded dog. I found it in a charity bin at that library sale. I put it in my stack. And that whining little Jewish nerd ran off with it when my back was turned."

"Maybe he didn't like you calling him a Jewish nerd."

Loeffler planted his hands on his knees with a sigh. "I'd hoped for better from a man like you, Harry. I'm truly disappointed."

"Because I don't call Jews names?"

"Because you're missing the big picture."

I could smell another hobbyhorse trotting onto the field. So I tried scaring it back to the stable with a blanket, even though I knew it was too late.

"You're not going to start spouting Nietzsche, are you?"

"I been known to tap the keg," Sherwood Loeffler said with a grin. "I'm no bigot, Harry, in spite of what you're thinking. I just don't much cotton to what I call the politenesses of this goddamn century. There's a pernicious idea hidden behind all that mind-your-mouth civility—an absurd notion that we inherited from the

Enlightenment that all men are, indeed, deserving of equal respect. It just ain't so. No more than the equally stupid notion that we all got the same rights. Who says? It's just a way we act and, in the long run, it causes nothing but harm because we end up lying to ourselves about our own patently unequal natures. We gotta clean out all them Enlightenment metaphors and them New Testament fairy stories and get back to what *is*. And what *is* is creative power—them that's got it and them that ain't. I'm not claiming that's the way it oughta be—it's just a fact. Men like Wagner and, yes, Nietzsche, remind us that this world is ruled by the powerful and that what's right is whatever increases and preserves that power."

Loeffler stared at me like I was blocking the view of his power base. "It take guts to live in a world like that. And being mealymouthed just don't cut it. Wagner knew it. He made art out of it. Something little toads like Leon Tubin just cain't see."

"Weren't you two guys friends for about ten years?"

"When someone stabs you in the back the way he stabbed me you cut the cord."

He sent his hand downward with a chop.

"Now you run on back to him and tell him I ain't gonna stand for any more of this foolishness. I didn't take his damn records. Hell, I got records of my own up the wazoo. I don't need his damn records."

"I suppose you have an alibi for last Friday night?"

He smirked at me. "Now, wha'd'you think? I was right here with my lovely wife Martha and our two adorable children."

I smiled. I couldn't help it. He was a bigot but he had a sense of humor. I got up to go.

"Come back any time, Harry," Sherwood Loeffler said expansively. "But if you're still working for Leon Tubin, bring a warrant."

# 5

## AND THAT WAS THAT.

It was half past noon and I had nothing left to do, except pay the retired building contractor, LeRoy Anderson, a visit. I felt a little like I was chopping wood for my wages, but I went ahead and phoned the man from a convenience store phone booth on Madison to ask him if I could come out and talk.

"Come ahead!" he said with what was becoming a chillingly familiar note of enthusiasm in his voice. "We'll put on some music, maybe."

LeRoy Anderson lived in what was once the sedate, old Jewish neighborhood of Roselawn. Over the past two decades it had slowly become a sedate, old mixed neighborhood. Older Jewish families. Russian émigrés. Black professionals. Well-to-do retirees like LeRoy. And a smattering of Hasidim, who strode the bleak, windy sidewalks in black suits and round black hats, like grave, wandering seminarians. I passed several of them—and a couple of black kids bouncing a basketball—as I searched for LeRoy Anderson's house. I eventually found it tucked away at the end of a narrow side street lined with colonials and bare-limbed, snow-dappled elms.

LeRoy was waiting for me at the front door of his handsome two-story, brick home—a cheerful-looking black man of no discernible age, wearing a checked tam and smoking a stubby cigar. He had a round, high-cheeked face the color of cherry wood, lively eyes, and a smile that was so broad and earnest it made me smile back at him.

"C'mon in," he said, waving me through the door like an impresario. I followed his arm into a short hallway which opened onto a living room on the left and a dining room on the right. A grandfather clock the size of a stuffed bear stood beside the door. LeRoy took my coat and hung it on one of the finials of the clock.

"So Leon's got his nose all open about them records," he said with a massive chuckle. LeRoy Anderson pulled the cigar out of his mouth as if it were plugging him up, and laughed some more. "These white boys kill me. Him and that too tall drink of water been feuding ever since I met 'em."

"They've had fights like this one before?"

LeRoy Anderson eyed me incredulously. "Now you got to know that they have—you being a detective and all. It's just like these two boys I used to hire in my construction business. The one of them, a black fella from Jamaica, says 'Yes,' and this other boy, big white boy from Tennessee, says 'No.' That's all they do from sunup to sundown. 'Yes/No' we called 'em."

"What happened to them?"

"Black fella from Jamaica pulled a pistol outta his lunch box and shot the white boy dead. He went and said 'No' one time too many." LeRoy shook his head. "That's a true story."

"It's not a particularly comforting one."

He threw his hand at me in disgust. "Oh, them two jackasses you're dealing with haven't got the guts to shoot off anything but their mouths. They're just blowing smoke up each other's ass, see who hops the highest."

"So you don't think Loeffler had anything to do with the theft?"

"Hell, no," he said. "Plenty of people know about Leon's records. Lord, he's cheated half the folks in the city out of 'em—him and that big tall ass, Sherwood. They go on over there to Kentucky and steal them off them hillbilly boys for a quarter apiece, then brag about how they done bested them—and each other." LeRoy arched an eyebrow. "Now some of those hillbilly boys *do* hold grudges, and they ain't all as dumb as Sherwood and Leon think. I worked with 'em so I know what I'm talking about."

"Then the thief might have been someone Leon bought records from?"

"Just as like."

"You thinking of anybody in particular?"

He laughed. "As many people as those two robbed?"

LeRoy Anderson made an abashed face, as if he'd

forgotten his manners. "Here I got you standing in the hall all this time, and didn't even offer you a chair. You go on in the living room there. I'll get us some drinks."

He started up the hall to a dark kitchen. "Beer or whiskey?" he called out over his shoulder.

"Beer," I called back.

The living room—a foursquare box furnished in mahogany and overstuffed, floral-print furniture—was as neat as a barracks. Too neat, I thought, as if LeRoy only used it for strangers or for show. On the right-hand side of the room a fire blazed in a small screened fireplace. A row of framed photographs were arranged on the mantel above it. I took a look at the photos while I waited for LeRoy to come back.

One of them pictured LeRoy in an army uniform, circa World War II. He'd put on some weight in the close to fifty years since the photo was taken and lost a dapper mustache he'd once cultivated, but he still looked surprisingly like the man in the photo, although he had to be close to seventy by now. Next to the army photograph there was another photograph of LeRoy and a pretty black woman in a silk dress. I was looking at it when LeRoy came in, holding a tray with two cans of beer and two mugs on it.

"That'd be my wife, Estelle," he said, putting the tray down gently on a coffee table. "She died of cancer in 1972. Estelle was the only woman in my life, 'cept for my mother. She died too, 'bout fifteen years back."

"So you're a bachelor now," I said, taking the glass of beer he handed me.

"I'm just a tired old man, mostly," LeRoy Anderson

said. "But I keep myself busy. Past twenty years I found something to stay busy with."

"What's that?"

"Stereo," he said with a big grin.

We had a beer and another. And before I knew it I was working on a six-pack. By then we'd moved down to the basement, where LeRoy kept his stereo.

The basement was LeRoy with his hair down, in his underwear, sitting on an old vinyl-covered couch with a beer in his hand and a salad bowl of mixed nuts on the folding plastic TV table, puffing on a stogie and listening to his music. The basement was as jumbled as the living room had been neat—pieces of old equipment, loose wire of every gauge and color, Maxwell House coffee cans full of resistors and capacitors littered the floors. And then, of course, there was The System. In LeRoy's case it consisted of two small oddly shaped boxes, finished in piano black, sitting on pillars that elevated them about three feet off the floor.

"Electrostats?" I asked him.

"Heck, no," he said with disgust. "Those damn things don't have no body or sock. I guess they're O.K. for the fairy dust stuff that Loeffler and Tubin play. But if you want to hear a trumpet and a drum set sound like a trumpet and a drum set you got to have cones."

Tiptoeing daintily through the crap on the carpet, LeRoy flipped the switch on a huge gray box the size of a baby's coffin.

"Where's the turntable?" I asked him.

"Don't use no turntable," he said over his shoulder. "Records are dead, man. I listen to CD's."

"I thought they weren't as good as records."

"Who told you that? Leon? Shit, you want to hear real? Listen to this."

He put on a CD of a motorcycle starting up. It did, in fact, sound very much like a motorcycle starting up, although I couldn't help thinking that if LeRoy had heard the same sound outside in the street of an evening he would have had a hemorrhage.

"Great!" I shouted over the popping pistons. "Maybe you could turn it down a notch."

"Wait a second," he shouted. "Just want you to hear one other cut."

The motorcycle wheeled off with a roar, and a herd of cows came stampeding down the street in its wake. There were cowboys, too, yipping and cracking whips over the mooing herd.

"Very realistic," I said.

LeRoy Anderson looked well pleased. "Ain't no way their puny little systems gonna produce dynamics like this."

To my relief the herd wandered off the left speaker and music came on the right—movie music from some TV western whose name I'd forgotten. *Sugarfoot* or *Cheyenne* or *Texas John Slaughter*. It was a heck of a lot better than the stampede. And when my ears stopped ringing I realized that LeRoy had a point. His system did sound fuller and more dynamic than those of Leon and Sherwood Loeffler, but not as transparent.

"You got a minute?" LeRoy said, pulling a pair of cables out from behind the couch.

"Well—"

"Just take a minute." He went over to the baby's coffin, switched it off, then tore another pair of cables out of its back, ringing their little brass necks like they were a pair of copperheaded snakes. Bending down he took the new pair of cables and reconnected the amp to a CD player with a flashing display.

"Which cable d'ya like better?" he said, flipping the amp back on.

On came the herd again, stampeding with even greater clarity from one side of the room to the other.

"I guess this one," I shouted over the hoofbeats of the cows and the hoots of the cowboys. "It's clearer."

"H'm," LeRoy said ominously.

We were working our way through the fourth set of interconnects and fifth can of beer when the first of Le-Roy's visitors arrived. A white guy with a beard, all bundled up in a heavy shearling coat, popped up at the foot of the staircase—I hadn't heard him come down the stairs over the roar of the herd—and just stood there with a moony look on his face, as if he were waiting for a bus or a stray heifer.

"Hey, there, Thompson," LeRoy said when he noticed him. "Harry, this is Paul Thompson."

I nodded at him.

"'Scuse us a second, won't you?"

LeRoy took Paul Thompson into a little alcove at the foot of the stairs. I couldn't hear what they were saying over the roar of the stereo. But about five minutes later Thompson started back up the stairs, holding a cardboard shipping box for a brand-name VCR. The moony look was gone and he was smiling.

LeRoy came back in the room and sat down on the sofa again.

"Just taking care of a little business," he said daintily.

"You sell stuff, LeRoy?"

"I buy and I trade," he said. "It keeps me hopping."

It did, too. In the space of an hour three other lonely guys made their ways down LeRoy Anderson's staircase—to get their fixes of video or stereo equipment. Old tube amps, fat speaker cables, a funny-looking record clamp, another VCR. All sorts of crap climbed back up the stairs with them. And all three men looked happy as clams.

A couple of beers and interconnects later a young black man in a leather jacket, dark sunglasses, and a Big Apple cap came down the stairs into the basement.

"Hey, pops," he said in a jittery, high-pitched voice. "Who's the ofay?"

"Watch your mouth," the old man said, but I could tell from his face that he enjoyed the kid's nerve.

"You gonna sell me that amp?"

"You got the cash?"

"I'm gonna put it on plastic," the guy said.

"Yes, you are," the old man laughed. "We don't take plastic at this store, Philo." Turning to me, he said, "This here is Philo Ives. Philo, meet Harry Stoner. Harry's a detective. He's helping Leon find his lost records."

Philo Ives threw his hands to his chest, palms up, in a gesture of surrender. "You steal them records, old man? You stealing again?"

"You watch your mouth or I'll get out my gun."

"Wouldn't want that, no." Philo walked over to the couch and sat down. He moved with a kind of nervous jerk in his step, like an ex-fighter or a crack head. And when he sat down he stayed in motion like a mobile—feet tapping, head bobbing, hands rustling over his pants legs as if he couldn't get enough of the feel of the cloth.

"Philo's a musician, Harry," LeRoy said. "He blows sax in a combo down at the Blue Wisp."

"You gonna sell me that amp or what?" Philo said, ignoring me. "Ain't anybody else gonna buy that piece of junk for what you're asking."

"You gotta have the green," LeRoy said, rubbing his fingers together.

"It's just gonna sit there and rot, old man. When it could be playing in Philo's crib."

"It ain't eating nothing," LeRoy said placidly. "You come up with the cash and you can walk it on out of here like your pet pig."

Philo grunted. "Why you dissin' me in front of this ofay? I'm good for the green."

Turning my way for the first time Philo pulled his shades halfway down his nose and peered, yellow-eyed, over the top of the lenses. "You a detective, huh? A stereo detective. Think I'll hire you to find my old lady."

He started to laugh.

LeRoy laughed too. "She ran off with his amp, Harry. Left the boy without sound."

"That's just why you gotta give me that amp there."

"Can't do it."

Philo rocked back hard against the couch. Reaching into his leather jacket he pulled out a stout wad of bills wrapped in a rubber band. "All right. Just this one time." He peeled off four hundred dollars' worth and handed it over to LeRoy.

"Take her away," LeRoy said, with a sweep of his hand.

"Don't have to tell me to take nothing away, old man. When something's mine I'll do what I want with it."

Philo Ives stood up, unfolding like a jackknife. "I'll come back and get it tomorrow."

And as quickly as he had come he was gone.

LeRoy turned to me with an amused look on his face. "He's a character. One of them fast-talking New York boys. Helluva musician though when he bothers to play. Got a real sweet tone."

"Where's he get that kind of money?"

LeRoy's face went blank. "Wouldn't know nothing about that, Harry."

≡≡≡≡≡≡≡

The tenth beer finally did me in. Dragging myself up the stairs I headed down the hall for the front door, with LeRoy trailing tipsily behind me. It had been an odd afternoon. And LeRoy Anderson had turned out to be an odd and appealing man. I didn't know where he got the stuff he was selling out of his basement. I didn't know if characters like Philo Ives and Paul Thompson were his usual clients. I didn't care.

I liked the old man for his energy and his enterprise. Stereo really had kept him young.

"You ever want to get into a system," he said, clapping me on the shoulder. "You let me know, hear?"

"I don't carry a wad of hundreds."

"We'll find one just your size."

I pulled my topcoat off the clock and tried putting it on. LeRoy had to help me with one of the sleeves—I was that drunk. "If you hear anything about the records, you let *me* know, O.K.?"

"Will do."

Before I left LeRoy gave me one last piece of advice concerning Leon and Sherwood. "I been knowing Leon since he and Sheila moved here in '80, and Sherwood near as long. Now, Leon, he can be a pain-in-the-ass. Always talking fast, whining about not getting his due. But he's a good soul at bottom, just a little sneaky. Sherwood's half a redneck who ain't quite comfortable being a whole one. He's a slow-talker but he talks long. And if he ain't as sneaky as Leon is he's just an inch away. These two boys been playing chicken with each other for ten years. Sometimes Leon comes out ahead and sometimes Sherwood does. I don't know who's gonna win this round. But far as I'm concerned it's still the same fight. Leon's making trouble for Sherwood. Wouldn't surprise me in the least if Sherwood starts doing the same to Leon."

LeRoy Anderson didn't know it—neither did I at that moment—but as it turned out he couldn't have been more right.

# 6

**I WAS FAR TOO LOADED** to go back to the office, so I went home—creeping down Reading Road at twenty-five miles an hour, then cutting over Martin Luther King to Jefferson and Calhoun. It was only half-past three so I didn't have the usual problem of finding a parking place on Ohio Avenue. There was an open slot right in front of my brownstone apartment building. I pulled into it and just sat there in the Pinto for a few seconds staring drunkenly at the baleful, smoky eyes of the brownstone's bay windows and the white picket brow of widow's walk arching above them, like Thurber's cartoon of home. I tried to remember the last time I'd come back to my apartment, crocked, at three-thirty of an afternoon, after spending two and a half hours listening to music and drinking beer with a stereophile. College, maybe. Twenty-five, thirty years past.

I managed to clear my head long enough to get out of the car and stagger up the short flight of front stairs and down the sidewalk on the right side of the building. As luck would have it the young woman who lived in the apartment above mine—a pretty grad student named Martina Kaufman—was coming down the walk as I was heading up it. We did a little do-si-do to avoid each other, which made my head spin. My stomach started to churn, too. All the beer that LeRoy Anderson had fed me was beginning to mix unhappily with the corned beef and greasy potato *latkes* I'd had for lunch. What I needed to do was lie down—or fall down. But a nice drunken snooze was not in the cards.

A folded piece of white paper was stuck in my door, wedged between the jamb and the door frame. I pulled it out as I fished through my pocket for the house keys. It was a note written in a frantic hand.

2:45 P.M. I have been trying to get you on the phone for hours. S.L. has broken into the basement again and stolen more records. Call me as soon as you can—or come directly to the house. I've left messages on your office machine and your home machine. DO NOT CALL THE POLICE UNTIL YOU'VE TALKED TO ME. The Nazi-dog Sherwood Loeffler will not get away with it.

The letter was signed, *Leon.*

Somehow I managed to unlock the door and walk down the short hall to the living room. The yellow message light on my answering machine was flashing but I didn't need to go through the messages, even if I'd been sober enough to remember how to work the machine. They were undoubtedly all from Leon and just as hysterical as the note. I sat down on the couch, picked the phone up off the end table, and tried dialing Leon's house. It took me a while—punching in the numbers was too much like addition. His girlfriend, Sheila, answered, and for a second I couldn't remember her name.

"Hello," she said.

"Hello, Sher—, Shirl—"

"Sheila," she said, helping me out. "Who is this?"

"It's Stoner. Harry Stoner."

"Oh yes," she said coolly. "The famous detective."

"Gotta speak to Leon."

"Are you all right? Your voice sounds strange."

"I'm a little drunk," I said with an abrupt laugh.

Sheila laughed along with me. "There are worse things to be. Leon isn't here. He went out—looking for you, I think. There's been another break-in."

"I heard. Tell 'im." I felt my head start to spin. "Tell 'im be over soon as I can."

I hung up, lurched down the hall to the bedroom, and collapsed on the mattress.

═══

About an hour later, when I could sit up again without setting the room in motion, I made my way through the living room into the kitchen. I tried brewing a pot of coffee in the machine that Jo had given me for Christmas, gave up and just poured hot tap water into a cup of instant crystals. I was still drunk—and sick—after choking down three cups of Folger's best. But I could drive. And I had the feeling that the sooner I got over to Leon's house the better. The note he'd left had sounded nuts.

I bundled myself up in a heavy scarf and overcoat but the late afternoon cold cut through them before I was halfway down the front stairs. I was trembling by the time I got to the car. The worst of it was that I knew the goddamn heater in the Pinto wouldn't come on for a good ten minutes.

I started off anyway—head swollen, limbs trembling, sick to my stomach. The radio in the car was set to classical 'GUC. In the state I was in, the Brahms *Alto Rhapsody* was no consolation. The soloist sang,

> *Ach, wer heilet die Schmerzen*
> *dess, dem Balsam zu Gift ward?*

"You said it," I said, flipping over to a talk show.

It took me almost half an hour to get to Leon's modest riverside bungalow. By then the sun had started to set behind the Kentucky hills, turning the ice on the Ohio River a brilliant, head-splitting white. The slanting light made the top of Leon's stucco house glow so brightly I had to flip down the visor to shade my eyes. I pulled up in the driveway and noted, with alarm, that there were no cars in the garage.

Sheila Mozkowski answered the door. She was dressed just as she'd been the night before—in a white shirt and black leotard. But this time she didn't look drunk. I did.

"Your breath smells like Pabst's," she said, making a face.

"It's a new cologne. Where's Leon?"

"Like I told you on the phone, he went out looking for you."

"What happened?"

The woman cocked her hands on her hips and sighed. "Better come in—this may take a while."

I went into the barren living room with its one piece of furniture and its trove of stereo gear. The TV was going, set to a talk show. Sheila flipped it off with the remote control and flopped down on the couch.

Giving me a look she said, "You can sit, too. I won't crawl in your lap or anything."

I sat down beside her.

"I guess I should apologize for last night," she said, without sounding apologetic. "I'd had a few too many, and I was pissed off."

"About me?"

She nodded.

"How come?"

"Money. I think Leon's wasting it on you. You probably don't know this, but he only makes about ten thousand a year from his teaching job. Maybe another ten selling records."

"I would've thought more than that," I said, remembering the wad of cash he flashed in my office.

Sheila Mozkowski snorted with disgust. "He would make more if he sold all the records he buys. But he doesn't sell them. He keeps the goddamn things. Between what he brings in and what I make part-time at the bookstore we have about thirty, thirty-five grand coming in. Half of that goes to records and stereo equipment. The other half to rent, heat, and food."

"So I'm a luxury."

"Luxury, hell. Look at what I'm wearing." She plucked at the cheap cotton fabric of the shirt. "I've got a couple blouses in the closet. A few skirts for work, two pair of jeans, and one ratty cocktail dress I stole from my last singing gig. Get the picture?"

"Yeah."

"We can't afford you, Stoner," she said, folding her arms at her breasts. "It's that simple. How much cash did Leon give you, anyway?"

"Five hundred bucks," I said guiltily.

The woman groaned as if I'd punched her. "Five hundred bucks!" she said. "Five hundred! That weaseling son-of-a-bitch! Where'd he get five hundred bucks?"

"He had a lot more than that, I think. A big wad of hundreds."

The woman's face turned purple with wrath. "Excuse me a second," she said, in a barely controlled voice.

She got up and went through the dining room into what I assumed was the kitchen. After a moment I heard the clink of ice cubes in a glass, and Sheila Mozkowski came back into the room, holding two Cokes in her hands. Whatever had been bothering her had apparently stopped bothering her, because she was smiling apologetically.

"Sorry," she said, handing me a Coke. "It's just that we keep some money around for a rainy day and I thought maybe Leon had spent some of it on you."

"Did he?" I said, feeling even guiltier.

"Not enough to matter," Sheila said, waving her hand dismissively. "I shouldn't have gotten worked up. It's just that when you live on a budget for a long time, you get kind of defensive about how you ration out the extra bread. And I have some of it earmarked to use for my comeback."

"Comeback?"

"I've got a singing gig lined up," she said, sipping at her Coke, "if I can ever get enough together to buy a couple of decent dresses and some PA equipment."

"Leon told me you were a singer."

She laughed. "He makes it sound like grand opera. I used to sing with a rock band back in the seventies. Last few years it's been a weekend here and there at the Ramada Inn."

Sheila Mozkowski was beginning to come into focus. The brass, the booze, the hands-on sexuality suddenly made better sense. What still didn't make sense was how she'd ended up sticking with Leon Tubin for thirteen years. As meal tickets went he was a damn poor choice. And given her looks she could easily have done better. The only answer was love—the oldest answer in the book. And the most improbable.

"Oh hell," the woman said, sighing. "I'm not gonna make a comeback. It's just a dream I have. I had a little luck early in my career and developed a taste for attention that I've never quite gotten out of my system. But . . . it's better the way it is now. I was headed for disaster before I met Leon—fast company, bad company. I'd end up in the same hole if I ever started back again. Only now we got crack and AIDS and tuberculosis and all sorts of new ways to kill yourself. Not like when we were kids, huh?"

I nodded. "I don't know what I'd do if I was young

today. It's gotta be rough—all those raging hormones and no place to go."

"Oh, I still got the hormones," Sheila said with a laugh. "I guess it's just lucky I *don't* have a place to go. Leon honest-to-God rescued me from myself. It's something I'll always owe him for. You know, something you can't pay back, although every once in a while I give it a try."

She turned her head away from me and stared wistfully at the gigantic loudspeakers. "So what if it gets a little dull around here sometimes between the records and the stereo? I get to listen to the music and read my mysteries." She patted the detective story by the woman from Nome, which was still sitting on the end table. "What's five hundred bucks, anyway?"

"I'll give you the five hundred back if you need it," I said.

"Thanks, but I couldn't take it now." She smiled a wilted smile. "It's decent of you to offer, though. You can do me one favor."

"What?"

"Get Leon off this stolen record kick. He's gonna do something foolish and land in trouble—I know it. And I love the little rat too much to see him behind bars."

"You think he's that crazy?"

"He certainly acted crazy this morning."

"What happened?" I said.

Sheila put the Coke down on the end table and curled up on the sofa, tucking her legs underneath her. "We went out for an hour around eleven—just down the street to a McDonald's. Leon felt bad about the way things had gone last night so he boosted me to a $1.98 breakfast. Big spender. He thinks he can buy his way back into my bed with an Egg McMuffin." She laughed. "Actually it was kinda sweet. That's the way Leon is— sneaky but sweet. And Lord knows I was the one who shoulda done the buying.

"Well, we were only gone about half an hour. When we came home we had a little hanky-panky in the bedroom. Then Leon went downstairs to get a few albums for us to listen to. I was up here waiting for him to come back when I heard this shriek and a bang. I thought one of the bookshelves had tipped over on him. There's some composer that happened to—some old Jewish man named Alcord or Alkan. He was a Talmudic scholar and one day he went to get a Torah off a shelf and the whole bookcase tipped over and killed him. Leon loves telling the story. He thinks it's funny because it's absurd, but it scares me. Those records weigh a ton and one of the cases almost did tip over one day a couple of years ago. Leon caught it before it could fall but he broke his wrist. Ever since then I've been paranoid about the damn things.

"Anyway, I went running down the stairs, expecting to find him buried under a ton of vinyl, and there he was, standing in front of a shelf with a record jacket in his hand and this look on his face like . . . like he was going to explode.

" 'It's empty,' he screamed. 'My 90283 is empty.' "

"What's a 90283?" I asked.

"Some special record. A Mercury, I think.

" 'They're all gone,' he says, pointing to his shelf.

'That bastard Loeffler's gutted half my Living Presence collection.' "

Sheila Mozkowski passed a hand through her short blond hair, brushing her bangs back off her forehead and staring into space with a hapless look on her face.

"Of course there was no use trying to talk to him," she said. "He bolted upstairs and out the door. I heard the car start up and that's the last I saw of him since around noon."

"He stopped at my place at a quarter of three," I said, "and left a note in my door. He also phoned me a few times."

"I'm getting a little worried," Sheila Mozkowski said, chewing on a knuckle. "I've never seen him this pissed off. And I've given him some good reasons to get pissed."

"He doesn't have a gun or a rifle, does he?"

"Leon?" she said, as if that was beyond belief.

"Under the circumstances, I think I'd better call Loeffler."

"I think you should too. I almost did myself. The phone's right over there by the amps."

I went over to the phone and dialed Sherwood Loeffler's number.

There was no mistaking his big booming bass-baritone voice. "Yello."

"Sherwood, this is Harry Stoner. The detective who talked to you this afternoon about Leon's missing records?"

"Why, certainly, Harry. My short-term memory has not eroded to such a degree that I would forget your recent visit."

There was something going on in the background at Loeffler's place. I thought perhaps he was playing Wagner very loudly on his stereo, although one of the noises sounded suspiciously like a siren.

I took a breath. "You haven't seen Leon this afternoon, have you?"

"As a matter of fact I have. A couple of very burly policemen are just escorting him off my property at this moment."

"Cops?" I said, swallowing hard. "He's been arrested?"

"I should hope so," Sherwood Loeffler said placidly. "He tried to set fire to my house."

# 7

**AFTER HANGING UP** on Sherwood Loeffler I called Al Foster, my old friend in CPD homicide. According to Al, Leon was being transported to the downtown Justice Center on a misdemeanor charge of wanton endangerment.

"What the hell does that mean, Al?"

"Damned if I know. Was he waving a gun or a knife?"

"I doubt it."

"Well he must have threatened someone with a weapon."

I wondered if a shaded dog constituted a weapon. "Is he bailable?"

"Yeah, if the charge isn't kicked up to felony you can probably get him out this evening."

"Who decides the degree of the charge?"

"The prosecuting attorney," Al said, "in conjunction with the complainant, of course. If they go for felony you'll have to wait for bail to be set at a prelim."

It looked like Leon had delivered himself into the hands of his worst enemy—Sherwood Loeffler.

"I knew this was going to happen," Sheila said as she threw a winter coat over her shirt and exchanged her slippers for a pair of Totes. "How much you think it's gonna take to bail him out?"

"*If* we can bail him out it'll probably take anywhere from a couple hundred to a couple of grand."

"Isn't that swell?" she said disgustedly. "Just hold on a second."

She walked off through the dining room into the kitchen again. I thought she was going to tap her rainy day money for bail. At least I did until I saw a refrigerator light come on in the dark room. A second later the light went off, and Sheila came back through the dining room, holding what looked like a frozen lamb chop in her hand. It was something from the freezer, wrapped in aluminum foil. Without a word she stuck it her coat pocket, grabbed a baggy purse off the couch, and went out the front door. Before leaving I checked to make sure the garage and basement doors were locked—there was no sense in inviting more trouble.

It took us about a half an hour to drive from Saylor Park to the brand-new Justice Center—the nineties word for jail—on Central Parkway. Sheila hadn't said a word on the way downtown. And I didn't know what to say. I parked the Pinto in a lot on Main, right across from the bunkerlike building, and we walked the short block over to the entrance. It was fully dark by then and cold. The wind didn't seem to bother Sheila as much as it did me. But then she hadn't had ten beers for dinner.

"You think they'll let me see him?" she said as we passed through the smoked glass doors.

"You could ask."

"If you play your cards right they usually let you see them," she said cryptically.

"You've been here before?"

Sheila didn't answer me.

I went down the hall to the Clerk of Court's Office to arrange for bail, while Sheila tried to wheedle a pass to the upstairs lockup. To my surprise LeRoy Anderson was already standing at the clerk's desk, alongside a man I didn't know.

"Hey, Harry!" LeRoy said with a grin. "You come down here to see our boy?"

"Yeah. How'd *you* hear about this, LeRoy?"

"Leon called me up about an hour ago. Asked me to come down and bail him out."

"How come he didn't call Sheila?"

LeRoy chuckled. "Guess he didn't want her to know."

It sounded like a good guess to me.

I glanced at the guy standing next to LeRoy. He was a short, skinny white man with puffy gray hair, a large nose, and a pale, thin, hollow face turned silver at the cheeks with five o'clock shadow. He was wearing horn-rim glasses and a rumpled business suit.

"You two met?" LeRoy asked.

"I'm Dr. David Barber," the man with the puffy

hair said, holding out a hand and giggling as if his name were a joke around town.

I shook with him.

"Dave's a psychiatrist."

"Psychologist," he said, correcting LeRoy. "I'm a child psychologist."

"You're a friend of Leon's, too?"

The man giggled again, disconcertingly. But he cleared it all up when he said, "I'm a stereophile. Part of the club."

"Ah," I said. "Have you guys made bail yet?"

"We've been waiting on this peckerwood," LeRoy said, glaring at the clerk.

The man behind the counter looked up balefully from a computer screen. "I'm doing my best, bub. The trouble is your buddy hasn't been logged yet. They must have just brought him in a few minutes ago."

"Peckerwood," LeRoy said again under his breath.

The three of us went down to a small lounge lined with coin-op pop and candy machines. We each got a Coke and settled down in plastic chairs around a laminated plywood table. I hadn't seen Sheila on the way down to the lounge, so I assumed she'd worked some magic on the jailers. I had the distinct impression she'd worked that kind of magic before. I wondered how she planned on getting the aluminum lamb chop through the lockup's metal detectors.

"Neither one of you saw Leon, did you?" I asked.

They both shook their heads.

"This can't be very serious," Dr. Barber said. "I'm sure we can straighten it out with a little plain talk."

"This is jail, Doc," LeRoy said, shaking his head. "Leon ain't in here for no child therapy."

"A little talk might help at another window," I said to Barber. "Sherwood Loeffler is the one who brought this charge. And whether or not it gets prosecuted depends mostly on him. If you were to give him a call . . ."

David Barber giggled. "But he's insane."

I didn't really see where that was germane. "You're all a little nuts, aren't you?"

LeRoy looked offended. But Barber only laughed.

"Certainly. Audio is the last refuge of the obsessive/ compulsive. Last and best, I'd say. Who else but an o/c would have the patience to fiddle, hour after hour, day after day, season after season, with what is, after all, a sophisticated toy."

"I ain't no o/c," LeRoy said sullenly.

"It's not a bad thing, LeRoy," David Barber said, giggling. "Most of the great scientists and inventors were obsessive-compulsive personalities, along with many of the great artists in history."

"Yeah?" LeRoy looked a little mollified.

"We're creative minds gone haywire. Like magicians and alchemists."

"Is that right?" I said dubiously. "And what is it you're creating?"

"The illusion of a reality," Barber said with a gleam in his eye. "The illusion of music being performed by a great artist."

"That's a swell trick. But it's not much more than that."

"No, you're wrong. It's a good deal more than that.

Did you know there is a well-known scientist at MIT who insists that his students don't listen to stereos? And do you know why? Because stereo is a drug. A soothing, addictive drug. Animals respond to music, geriatrics respond to it, even schizophrenics have been known to snap out of years-long fugal states in response to it. There is a part of unalloyed magic in music that is transmitted by nothing else on earth. It can sustain you and elevate you in ways no one has ever been able to explain."

"It's good stuff," LeRoy agreed with a nod.

"I have no problem with that," I said to Barber. "But what does music have to do with stereophiles?"

"It's their raison d'être. No serious stereophile would be interested in the hobby without it. Goodness, if it weren't for the music we'd all be listening to recordings of railroad trains and thunderstorms and motorcycle races."

LeRoy flinched. "Some of those things are good tests of a system's transient response."

"Yes, but a steady diet of them . . ." Giggling, Barber shook his head. "The music is where we all start. The love of the music. It's that love which drives us to get closer and closer to it—to make the sound as realistic as we can. To make it come alive."

"It doesn't have anything to do with spending money, then?" I said dryly. "Or outdoing your neighbors?"

"A little," Barber conceded.

"A lot," LeRoy Anderson said conclusively.

Which brought us back to Leon Tubin and Sherwood Loeffler.

"As I understand it these guys have been warring with each other for years. If it wasn't stereo it'd probably be something else."

Barber nodded. "Psychiatrically speaking they are opposite personality types. Paranoid and schizoid."

"Yes/no," LeRoy said.

"How do you think we could go about defusing the situation?"

"Getting Leon's records back would be a good start," Barber said.

This time I flinched. "I'm working on that. But in the meantime do you think you could talk Loeffler into dropping the charges?"

"I doubt it. I will try, of course. But Sherwood really has been the victim in this deal. I mean Leon had the police after him and the newspapers and . . . you. In spite of his bluster Sherwood is a sensitive man, as vulnerable to abuse and insult as anyone else."

"I guess Leon's religion isn't gonna help, either," I said with a sigh.

"Oh, Sherwood's no Nazi."

"The hell he ain't," LeRoy said.

"I'm telling you he's not," Barber insisted. "He's built up an elaborate philosophical justification for bigotry. But it's only a defense mechanism he uses when he feels threatened."

"That 'defense mechanism' got a lot of brothers hung from trees," LeRoy said bitterly.

I left the two of them hashing it out and walked back up the hallway to the clerk's office.

"Got the bail ticket," the guy behind the desk said.

"How much?" I asked, reaching for my wallet.

"Five hundred bucks, but it's already been paid."

"By whom?"

"Some woman came down here—real pretty blond woman—with a whole bunch of cash wrapped up in aluminum foil. She posted bail."

That explained the trip to the refrigerator. Both trips, actually. The first time she'd been looking to see how much Leon had pilfered—or put back. It was an odd place to bank. It occurred to me that the wad that Leon had flashed had been a bit of a con job, designed I supposed to convince me that the little hippie was a solid, paying customer. Sneaky but sweet, as Sheila had put it.

I glanced down the hall trying to catch sight of Sheila Mozkowski and her tricky boyfriend.

"If you're looking for the woman," the clerk said, "I saw her pick some little, bug-eyed creep up at the detention office. They both walked out of here about five minutes ago."

"Thanks."

I went back down to the lounge and told LeRoy and Dave they could go home.

"I'll call Sherwood tonight," Barber said. "Maybe I can get through."

"You got more chance of getting through to David Duke," LeRoy said sourly. "You need a ride, Harry?"

"I gotta car outside, thanks."

"I wonder how the hell Sheila and Leon are gonna get home."

I wondered, too.

**8**

**I HAD NO IDEA** where Sheila and Leon had disappeared to when they left the Justice Center, although it stood to reason that Sheila would want a few minutes alone with her bailee. Sooner or later I figured they'd come back to Saylor Park. And since I still hadn't heard Leon's explanation of why he'd been arrested for wanton endangerment—or had a look at the basement following the second burglary—I decided to go back to their house and wait for them to show up.

For the second time that day I made my way out River Road to Saylor Park—a drive that was becoming as familiar to me as the drive from my apartment to my office. Happily the highway wasn't as treacherous as it had been the previous night when I'd almost slid into an embankment. In fact I could afford to do a little sight-seeing, past Anderson Ferry where the Ohio River came into view. A drowned moon, white as a cueball, was floating in the dark center channel. I stared at it through the side window and felt glad to be warm and moving and moderately sober again.

It was half-past nine when I pulled up in front of Leon's bungalow. The place was dark and dead quiet. The whole street seemed to be asleep. I flipped on 'GUC—a live broadcast of *La Bohème*—sat back in the seat, and waited for Leon and Sheila to arrive.

Time was slow and *La Bohème* was long. After half an hour of Rodolfo and Mimi I started to get restless. With the sick hangover mostly gone, I discovered that I was hungry again. Or maybe it was the fact that Mimi didn't have much to eat.

Since I didn't know how much longer it was going to take Leon and Sheila to show up I toyed with the idea of cruising around the block, trying to spot the McDonald's that Sheila had mentioned. In fact I was about to start the car up when I heard Leon's garage door open. I glanced quickly at the house—but the lights were still off. I hadn't seen any other cars pull up anywhere on the block. And no pedestrians had walked by. That only left the one possibility.

I'll be damned, I said to myself, straightening up in the seat. You got lucky.

I peered into the sunken driveway, but my view of the garage was largely blocked by the driveway wall. It was too damn dark to see much, anyway. However, I could hear someone moving about inside the garage. The burglar, if it was the burglar, must have sneaked around the hedgerow on the far side of the driveway wall, and dropped down onto the blacktop.

Popping open the glove compartment I pulled out my long-handled flashlight and my short-barreled .38 Airweight. I tucked the pistol in my coat pocket and stepped out of the car into the cold January night. The driveway was only a few yards away from where I'd parked. I crept down it pigeon-toed, trying to avoid making noise or slipping on the hard slicks of ice layering the blacktop. When I got to the level area at the bottom of the driveway I clicked on the flashlight and trained the beam on the garage door. The garage had been locked shut when Sheila and I left. It was partly open now—wide enough to let a normal-sized human being creep through the gap. I wasn't so sure about a guy the size of Sherwood Loeffler.

Crouching down I shone the flashlight through the opening, lighting up the inside of the garage. I could see a few cobwebs on the back wall, some fresh oil stains on the garage floor, and the bottom half of the door leading to the basement record room. That door was open.

I remember thinking, somebody else has got a key.

I ducked under the garage door—it was a tight squeeze for a man my size, probably impossible for a guy like Loeffler—clicked off the flashlight, and stood there listening for any sounds of movement. But the place was dead quiet. After waiting a few moments to let my eyes adjust to the dark, I walked over to the open basement door. There still weren't any noises coming from Leon's treasure house.

Taking the .38 out of my pocket I edged through the open doorway into the dark basement and clicked the flashlight on again. The beam lit up the huge bookcases on the walls. I cast the light around the room, touching on bookcase after bookcase full of records. If there was someone else in the basement with me, he was well hidden. I started for the light switch on the far wall when an object on the floor caught my eye. Lowering the flashlight beam, I leaned over to take a look. It was a Mercury record jacket with a picture of a mandolin on the cover. There was something else on the cover—a smear of dirt or oil.

I was just crouching down to take a closer look when I heard something creak and groan behind me with a sound like splintering wood. I whirled around on my haunches just in time to see a whole bookcase full of records come cascading toward me.

"Holy shit!" I shouted.

I threw up my hands, but the bookcase kept coming —records pouring out of its shelves in long, thunderous waves. A tidal surf of shaded dogs and Mercury hats.

I thought of poor Mr. Alcord or Alkan, crushed under his holy books. And that was the last thing I thought until Sheila Mozkowski woke me up with a sharp slap to the face.

━━━━━

I was still on the basement floor when I came to— the bookcase on top of my chest and records scattered like fallen leaves all around me. I could hear Leon keening over them somewhere in the room.

"My God," he was saying, "my God."

"Shut up," Sheila snapped. "Can't you see he's hurt?"

Sheila's face swam into view directly over mine. Blond, big-eyed and uneasy.

"Harry," she shouted. "Harry!"

She disappeared for a moment and I heard her say, "This is all your fault, you greedy bastard."

"My fault!" Leon cried.

"I begged you to let this thing go. If it weren't for your goddamn obsession with records . . ."

She leaned back over me with a wet washcloth in her hand, and put the cool rag on my forehead.

"We should call an ambulance. He could have a broken skull."

Now that she mentioned it my head hurt like a son-of-a-gun. For a moment or two after I'd recovered consciousness I hadn't been sure what hurt and what didn't. But as I came around I realized it was mostly my head—the back of my head, which had been concussed when I hit the floor. The rest of me seemed to be more or less O.K.

I must've groaned a little, because the woman's face bunched up anxiously.

"Harry? Are you all right? Can you speak?"

"What do you want me to say?"

Sheila Mozkowski laughed. Her wayward boyfriend Leon popped into view.

"You O.K., partner?"

"I've been better. Can you guys lift this contraption off me."

"Sure thing."

I heard them grunting and groaning. And once I heard Leon say, "Watch those records—they're

Bluebacks!" Slowly the weight of the steel bookcase was eased off my chest and legs.

I felt down my body with my hands. There were plenty of sore spots, but it didn't seem like anything was broken.

Bracing myself with my hands I sat up and something inside my head shifted like water in a fifty-gallon tank. I touched the back of my skull and winced.

"You've probably got a concussion," Leon said, looking concerned.

"I got cold-cocked is what I got," I said disgustedly. "Cold-cocked by a bunch of records. Help me up."

The two of them, one on either side, lifted me to my feet. Once up, I got woozy and almost went down again. But Leon pinned me against the wall while Sheila held an ice bag to the back of my head. In a few minutes I was steady enough to walk upstairs and lie down on the couch in front of the stereo.

"You want to hear anything?" Leon asked.

"*Shonda!*" Sheila hissed.

Leon blushed furiously. "I was just being hospitable."

After that they left me alone. I lay there for a long time on the couch, wondering whether I was going to pass out again and wake up in a hospital emergency room. For a good ten minutes there was a black vinyl disc spinning inside my head at about 78 rpm. After an hour or so it slowed down to 33, and I figured the concussion was mild enough to be safely ignored. Gingerly I worked myself into a sitting position and sat there staring at Leon's giant speakers until Sheila came into the room.

She was dressed in a muumuu and mules.

"How's the head?"

"S'all right. Where's Leon?"

"Where do you think? Down in the basement sorting through his fallen idols." She sat down on the couch beside me. "What the hell happened anyway?"

"I came back here looking for you two."

"We took a cab over to the impoundment lot to pick up Leon's car." Sheila gave me an abashed look. "I tried finding you to let you know, but . . ."

"It's all right," I said. "I managed to get inside your house anyway."

"How?"

"I followed the thief."

"You mean he was in here!" Sheila threw a hand to her mouth. "Was it Loeffler?"

"I didn't see who it was. He dropped the bookcase on me before I had a chance to see him."

"He must have been pretty strong to push that bookcase over."

She had a point.

Leon came wandering into the living room with a record jacket in either hand, like a deckhand holding semaphores. "It could've been worse," he said. "Only two of them were broken and neither one was a winner."

"Are you counting me, too?"

He laughed. "No. How's your head?"

"It hurts."

"I am sorry, Harry," Leon said. "I really am."

"He almost caught the thief," Sheila said nervously.

Leon looked shocked. "You're kidding? You mean he was in the basement with you?"

I nodded. "I had him cornered and I let him get away."

Leon's face turned red with anger. "That son-of-a-bitch Loeffler!"

"I don't think it was Loeffler."

"But you said he was strong," Sheila said.

"This guy had a key."

"That's impossible," Leon said. "Simply impossible. There are only two keys to this house. Sheila's and mine."

"How can you be sure?" I said. "You didn't buy this place new, did you? Someone could have gotten a key from the former owners."

Leon held up a finger. "Yes, but we changed the locks when we moved in."

"Did either of you lose your keys at some point or other? You said you lost things regularly, Leon."

"Hats, gloves, not keys."

I looked at Sheila.

She shook her head. "No. I've never lost my keys."

"Then he had a key made," I said. "But he had a key. Those doors were locked when we left. I checked."

Leon sat down heavily on the rug, dropping the records at his sides.

"I guess Sherwood could've had a key made," he said, working it out in his mind. "Or hired a thief who could make keys."

"Leon, it wasn't Sherwood. The garage door wasn't open wide enough for a guy his size to get in."

"It coulda slipped down."

"It wasn't him."

"Yes it was," Leon said truculently. "It was him."

"He did have Leon arrested," Sheila volunteered.

Her sudden support of Leon's harebrained theory wasn't helping things. But then Leon had had a rough day, too. And I guess she felt she owed him some support.

"Why *did* he have you arrested?" I asked Leon.

"It's a long story," he said vaguely.

"I've got time."

Leon glanced quickly at Sheila.

"Tell the man," Sheila said.

"Yeah, all right, I'll tell him." Leon pulled his legs up and rested his chin on his knees. "I guess Sheila told you about the missing Mercuries."

"902 . . . something?"

"Yeah, that was my Rachmaninoff Third with Janis and Dorati. It's a bit slow-paced compared to the Janis/ Munch on RCA, but the piano is reproduced superbly well."

"I think we can skip the capsules, Leon."

His face colored again. "I don't think you understand how important these things are to me. Until I found Sheila, music was the only thing I could count on to sustain me, to keep me going. Music and books. They were my best friends before Sheila."

He glanced up at Sheila Mozkowski, who smiled at him.

"It's like someone's been stealing my old friends."

"How many more of them were missing this morning?" I asked.

"Thirty-one," he said, fetching a sigh. "Thirty-one Mercuries. FR/1's and RFR/S's."

"Meaning?"

"First pressings. The most valuable pressings."

"Are you sure they weren't taken during the original burglary?"

"Positive," Leon said. "I went through the entire collection—twice on the Saturday after the first break-in. It took me all day. There's no question that someone broke in this morning and robbed me again."

"You thought it was Loeffler."

"I still think it was Loeffler," Leon said with an adamantine look on his face.

"Why?"

"Because the thief left the empty jacket of SR-90283 on the floor—just like he did with LSC-1817. It's Loeffler's calling card—one empty jacket, like a slap in the Jew boy's face."

I thought it over—with the 70 percent of my brain that was still functioning. "Has it occurred to you that somebody might want you to think that Sherwood Loeffler is responsible for the burglaries?"

"Why would somebody do that?" Leon said with an alarmed look.

"To divert suspicion away from him."

Leon chewed it over for a second, then shook his head. "No, I don't buy it. I mean anybody who'd do something like that would have to know how deeply Sherwood and I hate each other."

"Is that such a big secret?" I said with a smile.

"Among professional thieves I would imagine it is."

"I wouldn't be so sure this guy's a professional. It's easy to break into someone's house if you have a key."

"Yeah, but that would narrow it down to guys in the stereo club," Sheila said. "And I can't see any of them robbing us."

"You could see Sherwood Loeffler doing it," I reminded her.

"That's different," Leon said. "He's an anti-Semite."

"So you think this is a pogrom?"

Leon straightened up where he sat. "You know, it distresses me how casually non-Jews like you, Harry, dismiss religious persecution as paranoia or special pleading. Getting called a kike or a sheeny on a regular basis isn't fun."

"I don't suppose it is," I said.

"Yeah, but you don't *know* how it feels," Leon said bitterly. "You can't know. And it's not just Sherwood Loeffler who's acting like a jerk. Half this country has started calling the other half names. It's part of the Reagan legacy. One of that Teflon asshole's great gifts to America was the public rebirth of bigotry. He gave the right wing its voice and now they're trampling ordinary decency—what they like to tar as 'politically correct' speech—under the heel of their own brand of political correctness. They say they're only being honest and straightforward, calling a spade a spade, but what they're really extolling is the same mean, self-serving, grab-everything-that-isn't-nailed-down partisanship that characterizes everything else about the Reagan-Bush years. I've heard Sherwood himself talk about bigotry as if it were just plain common sense."

"So have I," I admitted.

"What happened to charity?" Sheila Mozkowski said in a small voice. "As I recall it wasn't the least of the virtues."

"We're in an era of bad feelings," Leon said, shaking his head. "And there's going to be hell to pay down the line—just look what already happened in L.A. And whenever there's hell to pay guys like me get it in the neck. Well, I'm not going to let that happen. At least I'm not going to sit still and let it happen. That's one reason why I went over to Sherwood's place this afternoon and . . . ended up getting arrested."

"Loeffler claimed you tried to set fire to his house."

"Fire!" Leon scoffed, as if it were no longer one of the elements. "I lit a goddamn match."

"Where?"

Leon buried his head in his knees. "In his anteroom. Near his record collection."

"You tried to burn his records?" I said.

"Now you sound like the police," Leon said, looking up at me miserably. "I didn't set fire to anything. I just . . . lit a match. Of course, he grabbed my hand and twisted it behind my back and had his Frau call the cops."

"I see," I said.

"He doesn't have a case," Leon said with a stab at what was fairly hollow-sounding bravado. "I mean it's my word against his. But it wouldn't hurt if you could prove he's been stealing my records."

I sighed. "And if he hasn't?"

"It wouldn't hurt if he had," Leon said.

# 9

**BEFORE CALLING IT A NIGHT** I went downstairs to the basement again and took a second look at what was becoming the Greyhound bus station of crime scenes. There really wasn't much to see. The room was still a wreck from the fallen bookcase, with albums scattered under just about everything—like a roomful of kittens. Leon had stacked the most valuable records in one spot. The others he'd left for the morning.

I dusted the back of the overturned bookcase and managed to get several latents from the struts and a whole hand and palm print off one of the side panels. I had the feeling the prints belonged to Leon and Sheila —from when they'd pulled the bookcase off my body— but I lifted them on to tape anyway. I also did a bit of fishing through the records on the floor, hoping to turn up the Mercury with the mandolin on its cover—the one I'd been looking at when the lights went out.

"Are you sure it was a mandolin?" Leon asked. "And not a lute?"

"No, I'm not sure," I snapped.

"You don't have to take my head off. The reason I asked is that the record you're describing sounds like *Ancient Airs and Dances*. It's a pretty famous Mercury. Valuable, too."

"That's just swell," I said, straightening up.

My back hurt from bending over the records and my head hurt from the fall. It came to me that I wanted to go home.

"Keep looking for it," I said to Leon. "I think it had some sort of stain on the cover."

"None of my records have stains on their covers," Leon said with asperity.

"This one did."

≡≡≡≡≡

I went home. Home was owed me. I crept along River Road like an old man in a Buick. The cueball moon that had held a chilly charm a few hours before looked like a floater to me now. The salted highway seemed dark and treacherous. And I didn't like the singing sound of the tires. All I wanted to do was make it back to Clifton without getting hurt—back to my apartment and a nice, warm bed.

It was well past midnight when I pulled up on Ohio Avenue. Naturally there were no parking spots near my brownstone apartment house at that hour of the night. I had to park on Warner and walk two and a half blocks into the teeth of the wind to get to the front door. But it was *my* front door.

I had just enough strength left before hitting the sack to brew a cup of tea in the kitchen, fill an ice pack with cubes, and play back my phone messages. There were about thirty left by Leon, from earlier that afternoon. One from Jo telling me what a great time she was having. And one from Dr. David Barber—the giggling psychologist.

"I talked to Sherwood this evening. He's willing to . . . reach an accommodation. You're to call him first thing tomorrow."

Happily, tomorrow was another day.

I curled up in bed with the ice pack on my head and the teacup on the nightstand. Set the Globemaster to a gentle, uncomplicated waltz by Oscar Straus. And was just drifting off to a well-earned sleep when the phone rang.

I practically pulled the thing out of the wall.

"Yes!" I said, sounding even to my own ear like a German officer in a World War II epic—pre-1940 when the *Wehrmacht* was on top of the world.

"Harry?" a small, squeaky voice said.

"Yes, Leon."

"You think you could come out to the house?"

"What now? Another robbery?"

"No." He started to cry. "Some guy came here and he, he took Sheila with him."

Jesus Christ, I said to myself. "He took her? You mean he kidnapped her?"

"Yeah," Leon said with a sob. "Sometimes it's hard to know with Sheila and men, you know? But she didn't want to go with this one, Harry. She scratched his face and hit him with her fists. But he took her anyway. I tried to stop him but . . . he beat me up."

"Call the police, Leon," I said. "Right now."

"I can't," he said. "The guy said I'd never see Sheila again if I called the police."

What could I do?

I pulled my pants back on—noting wistfully that they were still warm from when I'd taken them off—slipped into a fresh shirt, chucked the ice bag into the bathroom sink, and took off for Saylor Park.

By then I was to that stage of weariness where sleep seems like something for squares. I craved a state deeper than sleep—a state they didn't have a name for —like the Unknown Continent or the conscience of a conservative. Halfway to Leon's house it began to snow. It seemed just.

The snow was really coming down when I parked just beyond Leon's driveway for the third time that day. Well, actually, it was the next day. Sunday. I got out of the car and managed to pull a hamstring on a patch of ice at the foot of the front stairs.

I hobbled up to the door and knocked.

I guess I expected to see Leon with a few bruises on his face—maybe a black eye or a split lip. But he looked so much worse than I'd anticipated that I actually caught my breath. Someone had really worked the little man over. I mean it was a professional beating—the kind that loan sharks deal out to guys who don't make the vig. Leon's face was so puffed up that I scarcely recognized him. Both eyes were almost shut, his nose was clearly broken, and there were bloody holes in his smile.

"Jesus, Leon," I said. "We've got to get you to a hospital."

"I'm so scared for Sheila," he said. "I tried to stop him, Harry. Really, I did."

"I believe you."

The little man fell against me with a groan. "I don't know if I can stand any more."

I picked him up and carried him over to the couch, then phoned for an ambulance.

Before the paramedics came to cart Leon away to Jewish Hospital, he told me that Sheila had known her abductor. She'd called him by name, "Bob."

"Does 'Bob' ring any bells?" I asked him.

"Harry," Leon said, "I have so many bells ringing right at this moment I feel like a xylophone. It's no secret Sheila's known a lot of other men. I guess he was one of the crowd."

My guess was that he was something more than that.

"Did you see what kind of car he was driving?"

"A Cadillac. I don't know what year. I don't know about cars."

"It's a shame it wasn't a Mercury."

Leon laughed feebly.

"Did you get the license number?"

He shook his head. "It happened pretty fast, and I wasn't in the best of shape at the time. I think it was a

Kentucky license. PVA-something. I can't be sure. Both of my eyes were swelling up."

Leon coughed violently, and a comma-shaped curl of dark red blood leaked out of his mouth and down his chin. I blotted it off with my coat sleeve.

"I think he must've busted something inside," Leon said, trying to look brave. "I've been waiting all my life to say that."

"I think you've done enough talking," I told him.

"But I'm not kidding," Leon persisted. "All my life I've fantasized about getting beat up defending the woman I love."

I laughed. "You don't fantasize about winning the fight?"

"A guy my size?" he said. "I never figured it was in the cards."

As soon as the paramedics arrived they hooked Leon up to plasma and saline. As I expected they called the cops, too. There was no way to disguise a beating like the one the little man had endured.

As they were putting him on the gurney he waved me over to his side. Pulling me down close to his mouth he whispered, "Don't tell the cops about Sheila."

"Leon . . ."

"Please, Harry. I got my reasons. You have to promise me."

What could I say?

"All right," I said. "I'll wait."

A moment later they had him out the door. I watched through the living room window as the paramedics loaded the gurney into the back of the ambulance. It took off into the snowy night, flashers going, siren screaming. I thought the noise might wake up a few of Leon's neighbors. But not one light came on up and down the street. It was like the Neighborhood of the Living Dead.

I had to stick around and wait for the cops, but I wanted someone to be at the hospital when Leon arrived. The only person in Leon's circle whom I knew halfway well enough to call a friend was LeRoy Anderson. It was close to two but I went ahead and phoned the old man, encouraged by the fact that Leon himself had phoned him when he landed in jail that afternoon. To my surprise LeRoy sounded wide-awake.

"Just listening to a little tune," he said cheerfully. "I'm a night owl, Harry. Been that way all my life. What kin I do for you?"

I told him what had happened to Leon, and all the fun went out of his voice.

"Why, the poor little son-of-a-gun couldn't hurt a fly!"

"Somebody sure as hell hurt him."

"I'd like to meet that gent," LeRoy said in a steely voice. "I got ways of dealing with boys who do things to my friends."

"So do I," I said.

Leon had sworn me to secrecy with the cops, but not with his buddies—and LeRoy was clearly that. I went ahead and told him about Sheila.

"God Almighty," he said, sounding flabbergasted. "You say this guy took her?"

"Apparently so. You don't know anybody she used to hang around with named Bob, do you?"

I sounded stupid saying it.

"Just Bob?" LeRoy said.

"I'm afraid so, LeRoy. The name Bob is all I've got."

"Well, I can spread the word. Maybe somebody knows him."

"I'd appreciate it."

Before hanging up LeRoy volunteered to go to the emergency room to tend Leon—I didn't even have to ask. After finishing with the old man I phoned Al Foster at the CPD, who sounded a lot less alert than LeRoy had.

"Twice in one day, Harry. People will talk."

"I need you to run a license plate for me, Al. A Kentucky plate—PVA-something."

"That's all you have? PVA?"

"The car is a Cadillac—I don't know what year."

"What's gotten into you?" Al asked. "You sound all business tonight."

"Tonight I am all business. This is important, Al."

"I'll see what I can do," he said.

The cops showed up right after I'd hung up on Al. A couple of Hamilton County Sheriff's Department deputies who could have given a shit about Leon Tubin —or anyone but a relative with money or another cop. I went over the story of the beating, leaving Sheila out of it, and sent them on their way in less than fifteen minutes.

Once they'd gone I decided to search the house to see if I could turn up any Bob-like clues. I started in the bedroom—one of Sheila's favorite spots. There wasn't much to Leon and Sheila's bedroom—a mattress and box spring sitting on the floor, two orange crates on either side of the bed, and a deal dresser with a mirror top on the far wall.

I went through the dresser first. I found men's and women's underclothes in the top drawer, all jumbled together like loose socks. The second drawer had shirts and blouses in it, once again jumbled together. The bottom drawer contained socks and slacks and a couple of skirts.

It really was a sixties' bedroom. I'd been there, so I knew.

I took a look inside the orange crates and found a couple of books. *My Young Years* by Arthur Rubinstein on Leon's side. That damn detective story on Sheila's. There was also a marijuana roach on Sheila's side of the bed, curled up in the sparkling center of a geode.

From the bedroom I went into what I assumed was Leon's study—a little cubbyhole above the garage fitted out with almost as many bookshelves as there were record shelves in the basement. A battered oak desk sat by the window, with a computer on top of it. I found a good deal of music paper in the desk, much of it written out with notes. There was tax information in another drawer, and a pile of notes Leon had written to himself on yellow slips of paper. It was in the file drawer that I finally struck a small piece of pay dirt.

Hidden away in a folder labeled "Old Stuff" was a dog-eared snapshot of Sheila with four guys in bell-bottom jeans and tank-top T-shirts. A couple of the guys were holding guitars in their hands. Sheila was holding a tambourine. I flipped the picture over and found an inscription on the back: "The Music Lovers—September 1972." And beneath the inscription was a list of

names, presumably the names of the members of the
"The Music Lovers" band: "Sheila, Luddy, Mark, Roy,
and Bob at The Ludlow Garage."

The Ludlow Garage was a rock 'n' roll club that had
briefly flourished in Clifton in the early seventies. I
flipped the photo over and studied the faces. I didn't
know which one was Bob. I didn't even know if he was
the right Bob. But it gave me a place to start.

I tucked the picture in my jacket pocket and clicked
off the desk light. I had my lead. What I needed now
was a motive for kidnapping—and I had an inkling
about where to find that, too.

Leon's kitchen was just a few short steps from the
study. I went in, flipped on an overhead light, walked
over to the refrigerator, and opened the freezer door.
What I wanted to know was whether Sheila was keeping
any more aluminum foil–wrapped lamb chops in her
piggy bank. Storing money in the fridge somehow fit
Sheila's style—which was, as near as I could figure, a
weird mixture of the free-love, free-wheeling sixties and
the plaid-tux, bottom-line culture of a Ramada Inn,
with just a little county jail thrown in for seasoning. She
clearly knew her way around a lockup. Not to mention
the fact that she'd been kidnapped by a thug.

I fumbled through the Banquet frozen pot pies and
Dove ice cream bars and hit the jackpot—literally. At the
back of the freezer, right below the ice-maker, there
were three more aluminum lamb chops. I took one of
them out and unwrapped it. Inside was a brick of one
hundred one-hundred-dollar bills, still sealed with a
Federal Reserve wrapper. Ten thousand dollars on ice.

Maybe as much as thirty thousand, if the other foil-wrapped bricks contained the same thing.

Thirty thousand dollars—now that was a motive for mayhem.

# 10

**IT SEEMED A LITTLE RECKLESS** to leave thirty grand in the freezer, considering that a thief had a key to Leon's house. Of course, the burglar had confined himself to the basement record shelves up until then. But with nobody home—possibly for days—he'd have all the time he wanted to ransack the upstairs rooms. I knew I couldn't count on Leon's neighbors to keep an eye out —if an ambulance siren hadn't awakened anyone, the chances of them noticing a sneak thief were pretty slim. I decided to take the cash with me when I left, even though I suspected that I was compounding a felony.

It was 6:30 A.M. when I got back to Clifton. I stopped at Jewish Hospital to check on Leon, locking the aluminum bricks in the glove compartment before getting out of the car. I went into the hospital through the Emergency entrance and found a weary-looking duty nurse at the admissions counter who informed me that Leon had already been taken up to a semiprivate room. His condition was listed as serious. Which meant he was out of immediate danger.

"I believe a Mr. Anderson is staying with him," the nurse said.

"That's good. Would you tell Mr. Tubin that Harry Stoner came by to see him and that I'll come back later today?"

The nurse said that she would relay the message.

Day was dawning by the time I got to Ohio Avenue —a big purple and yellow parfait of a sunrise, the colors of poor Leon's face. I parked the Pinto on Warner again, took the aluminum bricks out of the glove compartment, and dragged them, and my aching body, the two and a half ice-cold blocks to my apartment door. I half-expected to find a kidnap note fluttering like a pennant in the jamb. But there were no notes.

This time I didn't bother with the answering machine—or my clothes. I simply collapsed on the bed and went immediately to sleep.

———

I had a strange dream about Leon and Sheila. We were at a rock concert at the Cincinnati Gardens, only there was no band playing. Just a guy named Bob spinning records like a DJ. He had a good line of patter, this Bob. At least Sheila and I liked him. Leon said he stunk. That pissed this guy Bob off and he started breaking records over Leon's head. The records broke right in two, draping down over either side of Leon's skull like Mercury's helmet. At first I thought the broken records were funny, then I got mad and punched Bob's lights out. But when I'd finished working him over Leon and Sheila had disappeared down a well—like the whirlpool of a B-movie blackout.

I was going to follow them into the vortex when a phone rang. "Hello?" I said. But the phone kept ringing. It was still ringing when I woke up, sweating, in my bed.

I reached over to the nightstand and put the receiver to my ear.

"Yello," a big, booming, bass voice said.

"Yeah, hello," I said groggily.

"Harry, my boy, you sound like you could use a pick-me-up. Were you out on the town last night, you rascal?"

I pulled myself into a sitting position, wrenching one arm out of the bedclothes. My head was hurting and for a second I didn't remember why.

"Sherwood?" I said.

"You were supposed to call me this morning, my lad. Did you forget or did our ikey friend get cold feet?"

"Your ikey friend is in the hospital," I said. "Someone nearly beat him to death last night."

"It won't work," Sherwood Loeffler said with a chuckle. "My mother didn't raise no stupid children, Harry."

"Yes, she did. This is no joke, Sherwood. Someone almost killed Leon last night. Whoever it was kidnapped Sheila, too."

"Great God! You're not pulling my leg?"

"Aw, for chrissake," I said and hung up on the oaf.

I tilted the clock back on the nightstand and peeked

at it with one smarting eye. It was twelve noon exactly. Which meant I'd had four and a half hours sleep—coming off a drunk, a concussion, and a kidnapping. Every little bit of me wanted to go back to bed, except for the one stubborn part that Leon Tubin had hired.

I swung my legs around onto the floor and waited for the bell knocker to stop swinging inside my skull. Something in the bedroom smelled fairly awful. It took me a second or two to realize it was me. I was still wearing the clothes I'd worn the day before. The armpits of my shirt were practically eaten out with sweat and when I glanced at the shirt front I saw spatters of Leon Tubin's blood.

I stripped down and walked across the bedroom to the john and into the shower stall, turning the water on full blast hot. After soaping up I stood under the shower head for a long time, steaming the sweat and the leftover booze and sleep out of me. I might have stayed there all day if the phone hadn't rung again.

I flipped off the shower, grabbed a towel from the rack, and, dripping wet, walked back over to the bed. It was Sherwood Loeffler again. Only he didn't sound like the same man.

"Harry, I feel just awful about Leon," he said in a just-awful-sounding voice. "I don't really wish the little fella harm, you know? He's just got this . . . contentious streak."

When I didn't say anything Loeffler cleared his throat noisily. "Well I guess we both got contentious streaks. Under the circumstances I will drop all charges against him."

"That's white of you."

"What hospital is the little fella in?"

"Jewish," I said—with a sneaking pleasure.

"Ah, of course. I'll make time to go see him this afternoon. Is there . . . is there anything I can do to help find the culprit?"

"Not unless you know an ex-boyfriend of Sheila's named Bob."

"Bob, you say?"

"Yeah. He might have played here locally in an early seventies rock band called The Music Lovers."

"I'm afraid I don't know much about that kind of music."

He said it like rock was a minority.

"However, some of the other members of our club might be able to help. Would you like me to call a few of them up?"

"That would be good," I told him.

"Where can I reach you if I make any progress?"

"I'll be in and out of my office downtown," I told him. "Or here at home."

"Got ya," Sherwood Loeffler said. He started to say something else—something apologetic about Leon was my guess—but thought better of it. "O.K., then I'll just get right on it."

I pulled some fresh clothes out of my closet and put them on while I toweled off my hair. A frisson of fear shot through me when I couldn't remember what I'd done with Sheila's aluminum bricks. But I found them, and my overcoat, on the couch, right under the living room window—thirty grand and I'd been too tired to do anything but drop them in plain view on the sofa. In the light of day that didn't seem like such a hot idea.

I put the bricks in *my* freezer while I fixed some coffee. After a cup or two, and a handful of aspirins for my head, I took the bricks back out and tucked them in my overcoat pocket. The only reasonable place to store that kind of money was in a safe. And the only safe I owned was in my downtown office. Which is where I went.

It was a bright blue glary Sunday afternoon—a great day for a subdural hematoma. My concussed head was killing me by the time I found the car on Warner. I was afraid to look at my eyes in the rearview mirror, afraid I'd see the oncoming stroke in my mismatched pupils. I fished a pair of sunglasses out of the glove compartment, which cut the glare enough to allow me to drive. I managed to ease down Clifton Avenue to the Parkway and up Race. By the time I got to the Parkade I was feeling like I might survive the outing. I left the Pinto dieseling in my usual parking spot and walked uptown to my office in the Riorley Building.

The safe in my office was a big, old floor-standing Mosler, sitting right behind my desk. I'd bought it for show—to give my clients a sense of security—but in the fifteen years I'd been in the business I'd only used it once for a paying customer, to store some stocks that he wanted to keep safe over a holiday weekend. The rest of the time I used it to secure confiscated weapons and the occasional bottle of single-malt Scotch.

Before locking the bricks away I took a look at the two I hadn't yet opened. Like the first one they were full of brand-new hundred-dollar bills. Thirty grand worth, all told. It was obvious that that kind of money shouldn't have been in Leon's refrigerator—or anybody's refrigerator. Sheila Mozkowski wouldn't have bothered to wrap it up like lamb chops and hide it behind the pot pies if there wasn't something funny about it. Funny enough to get her kidnapped or killed.

It was the only motive I could think of for Bob's late-night foray. Sheila was nobody's rich wife or daughter. She wasn't politically connected. Working in a bookstore she had no industrial secrets to spill. And no cache of drugs hidden away in the house—at least none I could find. She was nobody at all—just an ex-hippie with a seedy past, a weakness for stereophiles, and a shitload of money in the Amana.

Of course if Bob knew about the money it figured that he knew where it had come from. Maybe Bob had thought he had a title to it. Maybe that was why he'd worked Leon over like professional muscle taking revenge. It made me wonder how much Leon himself knew about the thirty grand. If it *was* illicit cash it would be a damn good reason not to call the cops. And in spite of the beating he'd taken and the danger his girlfriend was in, Leon had made me promise not to call them. He had his reasons, he said.

Going by the book that's what I should have done, of course. Called the police or the FBI. Only a little part of me—the same part that was working for Leon—was mightily afraid that if I got the Feds involved Sheila and Leon would end up in jail. On the other hand if I didn't call them, Sheila could end up dead.

I stared at the phone on the desk, pondering the dilemma.

I was still staring at it five minutes later when Sherwood Loeffler walked through the office door with another guy trailing after him like his noonday shadow. As large as he was Sherwood made most men look like his shadow.

"Didn't catch you at a bad time, did we, Harry?" Sherwood bellowed.

"Keep your voice down," the other man said, putting his hands to his ears. "Christ, it's like listening to a *fortemente* in a rehearsal hall."

The other one walked over to the desk and held out his hand. He was a refined-looking fellow in a smart blue sportcoat and tailored gray slacks. His hair was the bright, bluish silver of a newly minted dime and it had been styled carefully with hair spray and rinse to set off his classically handsome face.

"I'm Lawrence Peacock," the man said, shaking with me.

"I call him the Silver Fox," Sherwood said with a chuckle.

"Oh for chrissake, stop it," Peacock snapped.

"You know you're a dog, Larry. Look at the profile —just like Ravel or some other frog composer."

For a second I thought Peacock was going to swing on him. Sherwood certainly had a way of getting under the skins of his friends.

"For your information, Mr. Stoner, I teach music composition at CCM."

"Tell him about your girlfriends," Loeffler said, sitting down in a chair and stretching his long, bandy legs out in front of him. "All those pretty young girls running up and down the halls of the music school and Larry with that profile of his . . . go on, turn to the right, let the light catch it just so."

"You're intolerable," Peacock said, smiling in spite of himself.

"What can I do for you, gentlemen?" I asked.

"The Silver Fox there has some information you may find useful."

I turned to Lawrence Peacock. The son-of-a-gun actually did look a little like Ravel when the light was right.

"Uh, this is confidential and rather embarrassing," he said, lowering his mellifluous voice. "But a few years ago I had a . . . fling with Sheila Mozkowski."

"This was before she met Leon?"

Peacock cleared his throat. "Not exactly."

"I see," I said.

"Sheila is rather open with her affections."

"She ain't opened nothing for me," Sherwood Loeffler said with a snort.

Peacock shot him an ugly look. "It's bad enough that I have to confess this in front of you, with poor Leon half-dead in the hospital. You think you could manage to put a lid on it for a few consecutive minutes?"

Sherwood Loeffler zipped his lips shut with his forefinger and thumb, locked them, and threw away the key.

"*In*-tolerable," Peacock said.

"Getting back to Sheila."

"It started at one of our New Year's gatherings. The stereo club used to have New Year's gatherings before a certain party spoiled everyone's fun." He took a quick look at Loeffler, who patted his lips and gestured with his hands as if he were dumb. "Can you believe that I've stayed on speaking terms with that for ten years?"

"It must have been a trial," I agreed.

Peacock sighed. "Anyway Sheila was a little drunk—well, I guess she was more than a little drunk. And I was . . . receptive. We started up in Dave Barber's backyard arbor and kept seeing each other for about two months after that, before her conscience—and mine—got the better of us."

"Did Leon know about your affair?"

Peacock nodded. "Yes, he did. She told him about it. Apparently she tells him about all of her flings."

"He puts up with that?"

"He loves her," Peacock said, blushing. "And I honestly believe that she loves him."

"Touching," Sherwood Loeffler said, breaking his silence. "Don't you always find the remorse of an adulterer touching? It's always so . . . generous."

"You bastard!" Peacock shouted, half-rising from his chair. "At least I don't go around impugning people's religion or the color of their skin."

"C'mon, fellas."

Breathing hard, Peacock lowered himself back in the seat. "I am not an adulterer. And neither is Sheila. Neither one of us was married at the time."

"But you were engaged," Loeffler said, grinning.

Peacock slapped himself in the forehead with his right hand.

"All right, all right," Sherwood said. "I'll stop. Finish telling your tale. It could be important."

It took Lawrence Peacock a full minute to collect himself and pick up the story.

"During our . . . relationship Sheila told me a good deal about her past. One of the things she mentioned was that during the early seventies she had either lived with or been married to—I was never sure which —a musician named Bob Sousa. This Sousa played drums for a band in which Sheila was the lead singer. He was, she said, very rough on her. After the band broke up, she and Sousa parted ways.

"That one," he nodded at Loeffler, "tells me that she was abducted by someone named Bob. It may be that this Bob Sousa is the man."

"It may be," I said. "Did Sheila say she'd had any contact with Sousa after the band broke up?"

"No. I got the strong feeling she didn't want any further contact with him—ever. He had a habit of beating her up, the swine."

That part wasn't so good. But at least I had a whole name to go on.

"You've been a big help," I said. "Both of you."

Peacock stood up. "I'm going to go to the hospital to visit Leon. Are you coming?"

"I'll meet you there," Sherwood said.

"No, you won't. You haven't got the guts to face him."

Sherwood Loeffler laughed. "*I* got nothing to be ashamed of."

"Oh yes, you do."

"Imagine that," Sherwood said after Peacock left. "Here he's having sex with Leon's common-law wife, and he's got the nerve to upbraid me for my morals."

Stretching those long legs Loeffler got to his feet. It was kind of like watching a building collapse in reverse.

"Well I guess I'll head on back to the old homestead. Unless, of course, there's something else I could do for you."

"Like what?"

Sherwood shrugged. "I happen to be acquainted with a chap named Ken Rochberg used to run a rock club here in town called the Purple Eye."

"I thought you didn't like rock music."

"Oh, I don't," Sherwood said. "Ken's a stereophile."

"I should've known."

"I took the liberty of calling him before I brought the old fox down here to make his peace before God. Ken said he'd be around this afternoon, if you'd like to pay him a visit."

"Lead on," I said, getting up from behind my desk.

As we were riding the elevator down to the ground floor, I asked Sherwood Loeffler why he was going to so much trouble for a guy whose guts he hated.

"I don't hate him," Sherwood said. "It ain't Leon's fault he's a Semite and got a whore for a girlfriend."

"Semite, huh?"

"I'm moderating my passions," Sherwood Loeffler said.

KEN ROCHBERG lived in North Avondale on Rose Hill Circle. It was a lovely old neighborhood full of the kinds of houses that no one had been able to afford to build since the twenties—villa-like dwellings with tremendous square footage and tremendous heating bills. Rochberg's house was a mansion made of cut-stone inset with mullioned windows. The roof had the soft, undulating lines of a thatched roof but was, in fact, made entirely of shingles.

"It's called a Shaker roof," Sherwood said, as we pulled up in front of the house. "Queer, ain't it?"

"It's different."

"Ken's a little different, too."

I wasn't sure what to make of that until we knocked on the door. A thin albino man without a hair on his pale head or face answered our knock. He was wearing a black turtleneck shirt and black slacks that only accentuated the pallor of his skin. He smiled warmly at Sherwood.

"Hey, man, c'mon in. Is this your detective friend? I'm Ken Rochberg."

"Harry Stoner," I said, shaking his pale white hand.

The pallor had given me the impression that Rochberg was weak, almost boneless. But he had a good strong grip.

Rochberg waved us through the door into an atriumlike hallway with a huge staircase sweeping up from it to a second-floor balcony. A pretty girl with red hair and pale blue eyes was leaning over the balcony railing.

"You need anything, Ken?"

"We'll be fine," Rochberg said, waving at her.

The girl grinned and bounced off into one of the second-floor rooms.

"That's my wife," Ken Rochberg said, smiling. "You guys want to listen to some sound?"

"Why sure," Loeffler said, rubbing his hands together. "You got that old system cranked up?"

"I even put a little Wagner on the 'table just for you, Sherwood."

"This isn't exactly a stereo visit," I said.

Ken Rochberg's face fell a half an inch. "Oh."

"Harry here wanted to ask you a few questions, Ken. If you wouldn't mind?"

"No, of course not," he said, perking up—but not quite the full half-inch he'd dropped. "Is this about Leon?"

I nodded.

"Well, then, of course I'd be happy to help. Have you been to see him, Sherwood?"

"Not quite yet."

"I think I'll go tonight. You wanna come along?"

"Let me get back to you," Sherwood Loeffler said.

Ken Rochberg led us into a study the size of my entire apartment. Built-in bookcases full of books and records lined two of the walls. The other two were full of pictures and posters from the late sixties and early seventies—playbills, photographs, and memorabilia from the Purple Eye.

"My misspent youth," Rochberg said with a shy smile.

"Mine, too," I said.

"It was a time, wasn't it?"

"It was."

We sat down on a leather tuxedo couch that was as plush as kid gloves. Across from us a fire crackled in a giant fireplace with a Rookwood mantel that ran the length of the wall. There were bookshelves above the mantel and two pairs of tall, thin speakers on either side —well away from the fire itself.

"Electrostats," Sherwood said, giving me a nudge.

"What is it I can help you with?" Rochberg asked.

I said, "Do you remember a band called The Music Lovers?"

"Sure, I do. Sheila Mozkowski was their lead singer. They were our house band for about six months in '72."

"Do you know what happened to them?"

Rochberg put on his thinking cap. "As I recall they got a recording contract with Capitol and went out to L.A. But I don't think they ever cut a record, and Capitol eventually dropped them. I heard they had some personnel problems after that and ended up splitting up in '73 or '74. Over the last decade a few of them have drifted back into town. Sheila, of course. And Luddy Carter."

"How 'bout Bob Sousa?"

Ken Rochberg shook his head. "He's the real reason Sheila and the band never made it. That guy was a bummer. Always stoned on something nasty like MDA or dust. Always pushing other people around. And greedy as hell."

It sounded like the recipe for a kidnapper.

"Do you think this guy Luddy Carter might know where Sousa is?" I asked.

"He might. He was as tight as anyone was with Bob. You want me to give him a call?"

"Yeah."

Rochberg stood up.

"While we're waiting," Sherwood said, "how about some tone?"

"O.K.?" Rochberg said to me.

"Sure."

That brought him all the way back—the full half-inch.

===

As promised he played us Wagner, the first act of *Die Walküre*. Siegmund, Sieglinde, Hunding, the whole Volsung crew.

"Kinda appropriate, don't you think," Sherwood said, "after the Silver Fox's confession?"

I told Loeffler I had a little trouble fitting Larry

Peacock, Sheila Mozkowski, and Leon Tubin into the Ring myth. But he was only too happy to disabuse me.

"It's all myth, Harry," he said, shutting his eyes and running his hand over the melody like it was a tangible presence. "That's all life really amounts to, isn't it? Old stories we keep acting out on different stages?"

"Are you quoting Nietzsche again?"

"Sort of." He smiled. "You know sometimes I think philosophy is just a heap of dead ashes. None of your organized thinkers ever gets down to bedrock. Only your great artists go that deep. The stories they tell—that's where the real wisdom lies."

"But music doesn't tell a story," I said.

"Of course it tells a story. Are your ears stuffed up? Can't you hear what's going on?"

"It's an opera."

"It's drama, man. All music is drama and myth."

"What about a symphony or a piece of chamber music?"

"Same deal."

"There aren't any words."

"We supply the words," Sherwood Loeffler said.

Siegmund was hailing Sieglinde as his sister and his bride when Luddy Carter showed up. Down went the sound like a curtain, and Sherwood's spirits seemed to sink along with it.

Carter was a husky man in his mid-forties with a full brown beard, horn-rim glasses, and a bad hairpiece. So bad it looked as if a beaver had perched on his head. Like most people with pieces he kept patting and scratching and touching his wig in a vain attempt to convince everyone else that his hair was real.

Sherwood Loeffler laughed when he saw it, then turned away to avoid making eye contact with poor Carter, who knew—as people with hairpieces always know—that the laugh was on him.

"He woulda been better off with a gallon of Sherwin-Williams glossy enamel," Loeffler said, not quite under his breath.

The interview started badly and went downhill. Carter couldn't forget his wig. And even if he could have Sherwood wasn't going to let him. I had the feeling that Sherwood was suffering from *Wagner interruptus* and holding it against Luddy.

"What kind of name is that?" Sherwood said. "Luddy? Are you a Luddite?"

"I'm Episcopalian," Carter said.

I managed to get one solid piece of information out of Carter between Sherwood's jibes. Unfortunately it was a very bad piece of information.

"Bob Sousa's dead," he told us. "He got killed in a motorcycle accident back in '77."

My spirits fell—better than half an inch.

"You sure of that?" Sherwood said suspiciously. "Don't some of you hippies practice living burials and things like that?"

"What's with this guy?" Luddy said to Ken Rochberg.

Ken just shook his head.

"Hey, check it out, if you don't believe me. It made the papers here. Bob got drunk on Christmas Eve and drove onto an exit ramp of I-75, right into a semi."

"Very sensible," Sherwood said.

"Hey, he was drunk!" Luddy Carter said.

Luddy and Sherwood almost came to blows before the hour was out. But when Sherwood stood up, Luddy backed down.

"Let that be a lesson to you," Sherwood said, stretching to his full six feet eight.

It was two-thirty when I got the big S back to his Currier & Ives house in East Walnut Hills.

"I'm gonna stop at the hospital," I said to him. "You want to come along?"

"Oh, I think I'll wait till tonight. The little fella's probably sick of visitors by now."

"Suit yourself."

As he got out of the car I said, "You been a help, Sherwood."

He tossed a giant hand at me. "*De nada,* as them spics always say."

# 12

**IT WAS A LITTLE PAST THREE** when I arrived at Jewish Hospital. I got Leon's room number from a volunteer at the reception desk in the first-floor lobby.

"He's in room 1222 Ridgeway," she said, looking puzzled. "There must have been a shortage of beds last night because the twelfth floor is where they usually put the geriatric cases."

I followed arrows down a glassed-in corridor to the Ridgeway wing, past a long wall full of the usual banal industrial artwork—photographs of flowers and framed quilts and insipid abstract prints that were like Tums for the eyes. There was a bank of elevators at the end of the hall. I took one up to twelve, nearly running down an old man in a walker as I got off.

"Oops," he said, as if it had been his fault.

Room 1222 was at the north end of a wing of rooms

to the right of the central nurses' station. I knew which one it was without looking at the numbers because Le-Roy Anderson was standing outside the door, alongside a tall, balding man I hadn't met.

"Have you been here all night?" I said, smiling at LeRoy.

"Naw," he said, smiling back at me. "I went home and got some sleep once they settled him down. Just got back a coupla hours ago. Do you know Pavel Fleischer?"

The tall man held out his hand.

"I'm Pavel Fleischer," he said as we shook.

Pavel Fleischer had a trace of Middle Europe in his soft voice, and more than a trace in his long, melancholy face. Even when he smiled his eyes stayed melancholy, as if sometime in the past he'd simply laughed himself out.

"Pavel's an immigrant," LeRoy said. "That's how come he talks funny."

"I'm from Hungary. Budapest. My family came over 1968. So I'm practically American."

LeRoy chuckled. "With that brogue you ain't never gonna be an American."

"How's Leon?" I asked.

"Just fine," LeRoy said. "Running them nurses ragged fielding his phone calls. They're just now changing his sheets."

Inside the hospital room I heard someone groan like a sea lion.

"Jesus!" I said.

LeRoy laughed. "That ain't Leon. That's that Mr. Goldfarb they put him next to. He's ninety years old and they just give him a catheter that he don't much like. Fact is he keeps pulling it out."

"You're killing me with that tube!" a man shouted.

"Has it been like this all day?" I asked.

"Pretty much," LeRoy said. "They're gonna move Leon down to six soon as they get a bed."

A red-faced nurse came out the door of 1222 with a bundle of sheets in her arms and a fresh scratch on her cheek.

"You can go in now," she said testily.

"You go on, Harry," LeRoy said. "We'll wait out here for ya."

I went into the room. Leon was propped up in the near bed. Mercifully someone had drawn a curtain around Mr. Goldfarb's bed. Leon smiled when he saw me come through the door, and I saw the wires on his teeth from where they'd set his jaw.

"How ya doing?" I said.

"I been better," Leon said, although it came out through the wires sounding like "I b'bear."

"You got a broken jaw, huh?"

He nodded.

"Leon, I know it's tough for you to talk but I need to ask you a few questions about Sheila."

He nodded again, vigorously. "G'head."

"I been trying to run down the guy who kidnapped her, this guy Bob. At first I thought it might be Bob Sousa, the drummer who played in Sheila's band."

Leon shook his head, left to right. " 'S dead."

Great, I said to myself. I could've saved a couple of hours if I hadn't let Sherwood Loeffler drag me to a concert.

"Has Sheila ever mentioned any other Bobs to you? Guys she might have spent some time with?"

"M'be. Don' 'member."

"The one who beat you up—did Sheila say anything else that might identify him?"

"S'd D'troy."

"I didn't catch that."

Leon reached over to the nightstand and picked up a pad of paper and a pencil. He scribbled something on the pad and showed it to me: "She said 'Detroit.' "

"Detroit? Like the guy was *from* Detroit?"

Leon shrugged. "Dunno."

"Did Sheila ever live in Detroit?"

"Don' th'n so."

Bob from Detroit. That was a hot tip for the FBI.

"What did this guy look like, Leon?"

He started writing on the pad. After a moment he handed it to me: "He looked like Richard Wagner—only a lot bigger and without the muttonchops."

I laughed. "Sherwood will be so pleased."

Leon made a pained face—which in his condition wasn't difficult to do. Grabbing the pad back he wrote something else down: "I'm not kidding!"

I tried to picture Richard Wagner—a foot or so taller and without the muttonchops. The square, pouchy, brick-red face. The unruly hair, going gray at the temples. The cold, uneasy eyes and twisted, chewed-over mouth. If you put that package in a leisure suit with a wide-lapel shirt and wing-tip shoes, Wagner had the makings of a good German thug.

"How tall was he, Leon? What did he weigh?"

Leon scribbled on the pad: "Over six feet, and real

husky, almost fat." He grabbed the notepad back from me: "He had a tattoo on his right forearm."

"What did it say, 'Blood of the Volsungs'?"

Leon didn't smile. "It said 'Semper Fi,' " he wrote.

Bob from Detroit, an ex-Marine who looked like Richard Wagner in a leisure suit. It was starting to add up.

I had the feeling Leon was feeding me a line of bull. And I thought I knew why.

"Leon, I found the money in the freezer of your refrigerator. You know, the hundred-dollar bills wrapped in aluminum foil?"

"Frig'raor?" he said with an innocent look.

"C'mon, Leon, quit wasting time here. Sheila's life may be at stake. Where'd that money come from?"

"Dunno 'bout m'ny."

"I don't buy that, Leon. Sheila's been living with you for thirteen years, and you're telling me you never opened the freezer?"

Leon's lips trembled as if he was going to break into tears. He stared at me with an imploring look on his face. "Tellin' all I c'n."

"What can't you tell me? Did someone contact you, Leon? I know you've gotten quite a few phone calls. Did Bob call here at the hospital?"

"Bob called?" a man suddenly cried out in a demanding voice. "Why didn't someone tell me that Bob called?"

I looked around the room, then back at Leon. He pointed to the curtain drawn in front of Mr. Goldfarb's bed, then back to his temple, circling his finger in the classic sign for craziness.

I started to laugh.

"Na' f'ny," Leon said.

Picking up the notepad he wrote: "You gotta trust me, Harry. You gotta find Sheila before it's too late. And you can't go to the cops. I have good reasons."

I wasn't happy with Leon Tubin or his good reasons when I left the hospital room. I knew he wasn't telling me the truth, and I thought I knew why. The thirty thousand good reasons why. He'd had a day to think about what to do and had apparently decided to clam up until he heard from Bob—if he hadn't heard from him already. I didn't completely trust his cockamamy description of the kidnapper, which sounded like it owed more to his hatred of Sherwood Loeffler than it did to reality. And I didn't believe him when he'd denied knowing about the thirty grand.

Outside in the hall LeRoy and Pavel Fleischer were pretending that they hadn't overheard the conversation between me and Leon. At least Pavel Fleischer was.

"Who is this guy Wagner?" LeRoy said, after what he considered a decent interval of silence. "Is that like Robert Wagner?"

"He's a German composer," Pavel Fleischer said. "A Nazi."

LeRoy grew wroth. "You tellin' me a Nazi beat Leon up?"

"A guy that looked like a Nazi," Pavel said.

"I'm gonna get my magnum," LeRoy said, stalking back into Leon's room. "Case that son-of-a-bitch shows up again."

It wasn't an altogether bad idea.

I wandered up the hall to the nurses' station, with

Pavel Fleischer trailing behind me like a baby chick. Even after twenty-some years in the States Fleischer had the stranger's air of not being quite at home in a new town.

I found a girl at the nurses' station who'd been on duty all day—a pretty kid in a candy-stripe uniform.

"Have you been fielding calls for the guy in 1222?"

"Yes," she said. "He can't talk very well, so we've been trying to answer the phone for him."

"Do you remember getting a call from a guy named Bob?"

She laughed nervously. "What a peculiar question."

"Bob's a friend of Leon's," I said.

The girl thought it over for a second. "I don't remember anybody named Bob calling. There was a Caroline and a Larry Peacock."

"How 'bout Bob's wife Sheila? Maybe she made the call."

"We didn't take all the names, sir," the girl said, looking slightly bewildered. "And we didn't answer every call. Sometimes Mr. Tubin answered—or tried to."

"Thanks," I said, turning away from the counter.

"Mr. Stoner?" Pavel Fleischer was standing right behind me. He had a sad look on his long, pensive face. "I think I must tell you something. In private, please."

"O.K."

We went down the hall to a consultation room fitted out with a round wooden table and several chairs. Fleischer sat down at the table and pulled out a pack of cigarettes. He shook one out and half the pack came with it. Blushing he bent over and picked them up, shoving them back in the pack one by one.

"Oh hell," he said, tossing the pack on the table and putting his hands to his face. "I'm so ashamed. I don't know how to say this."

"Is it about Leon?"

He nodded, dragging his hands down his cheeks and pulling the flesh under his eyes with them. "This is awful. Leon, he was my first buddy when I move here. He teaches me about music and records. I wouldn't make a living if not for Leon."

"You're a musician?"

"I sell records. Like Leon. Records and other stuff."

"What other stuff?"

"Junk. Cameras, books, paintings. Anything I find secondhand. I go to estate sales, auctions. I have customers who will buy anything for the right price. Émigrés. Greenhorns, you know?" He shook his head unhappily. "This is so shameful."

I stared at him for a moment, wondering if he had enough arm to push a bookshelf full of records onto my head. He was certainly in an agony of remorse over Leon. And the robberies were the only things I could think of that might have caused it. "Don't tell me you're the one who's been stealing Leon's records?" I said.

Pavel Fleischer dropped his hands from his cheeks and slapped the table with his palms. "Me! Steal records from Leon! Oh, please. What kind of man do you think of me?"

His face twisted with disgust.

"I'm sorry," I said quickly. "It was just a wild guess. What is it you wanted to say?"

"It's about Sheila."

"You have some information about Sheila?"

He nodded. "I seen something—maybe it could be important. Maybe not."

"What did you see?"

"This guy Bob?" He swallowed hard. "I think maybe I have met him."

"When?"

"I buy records from him, maybe. Many years ago in Kentucky."

I started to get a little excited. "Go on."

"It is Sheila who tells me he's in town and has records to sell. I go over and talk to him. We meet in this motel by the river. You know this one? Big cylinder with the restaurant?"

"The Quality Court?"

Pavel nodded. "Yes. This is the one. Anyway I go up to his room and Sheila, she is there, too. I think . . . I don't know what I think. This guy, he shows me these records he's got. Says he was in the record business, you know—rep'd for one of the record companies. He says he would like to keep these records, but he is always in road. Besides he needs money. I say, 'Sure. I got money, you got goods.' I buy a hundred of them. Very reasonable. Then I say to myself, why doesn't Sheila tell Leon about this guy? I mean these were good records— shaded dogs, Mercuries. I'm not classical music lover, you know? But I buy them anyway. Later I found out why Sheila doesn't tell Leon about this guy."

"Why?"

"He was *shtupping* her is why."

"How do you know that?"

Pavel Fleischer dropped his head to his chest. "This is what is shameful."

He gave it a beat and said, "I am *shtupping* her, too."

**13**

**IT WAS BEGINNING** to look like Leon's little circle of friends had at least one thing in common besides stereo. It also looked like Sheila had a funny way of repaying her sneaky but sweet lover for saving her life.

To avoid future surprises I asked Pavel Fleischer if Hank Diamond—the one member of the club I hadn't yet met—had also been . . . *shtupping* Sheila Mozkowski.

"I don't think so," Pavel said miserably. "You don't know how ashamed I feel."

"It'll be our little secret," I told him. "Did Sheila tell you anything more about the guy with the records?"

"She says she has known him from before, in the seventies when he was performer. She says his name is Bob Adams."

"Did she mention whether he came from Detroit?"

Pavel Fleischer shook his head. "No. He talks with kind of Southern accent, I think. Like Sherwood."

"What did he look like, this Bob Adams?"

"He is a big guy, fat. Maybe he is forty years old. He has red hair, this guy, and a square face and blue eyes."

I hated to admit it, but it did sound as if Bob Adams looked like Richard Wagner.

"There was something about this guy I don't like. You go into so many strangers' house like I do, you figure out how to know if there is gonna be trouble. This guy, he was pretending to be nice guy. But his eyes . . . they're not nice. Also he did something bums me out—real bummer. We're talking about these records he has, and Sheila, she says something . . . I dunno what, but I think it is funny. Only this guy, he doesn't think it's funny, so he hits Sheila on the cheek. Not hard, but not like no slap, either. Sheila, she laughs, but I don't think it is funny. So, I leave."

"Did you ever see this Bob Adams again?"

"No. I don't want to see him again. Later Sheila tells me she isn't gonna see him no more either. She says he's just a one-night stand. Old times' sake. I tell her I am upset how he hits her, but she tells me 'I will handle it.' " Pavel Fleischer ducked his head. "Sheila is pretty good—best—at handling guys."

"When was all this?"

"I guess maybe three and half, maybe four years. Nineteen eighty-eight."

"O.K., Pavel. Thanks."

Sighing as if his heart would break, Pavel got up from the table. "I guess I should go back to the room. Someday I'll get enough courage to tell Leon. It is a bummer what I do . . . what I do to him. Total bummer."

"He probably already knows," I said reassuringly.

"It does not matter. *I* must tell him."

═════

I took what Leon and Pavel Fleischer had told me down to the CPD on Ezzard Charles. I found Al Foster, my dour friend on homicide, in his cramped little office, smoking up the usual storm. Officially they'd limited smoking at the CPD to certain areas of the building—just like they had everywhere else in the world. Al's office seemed to be the nexus of the world plan.

"You know I'm up to six packs a day now," he said with pride.

"Keep going, Al. Try for a carton."

"I ran that Kentucky plate for you."

"Yeah? Get anything from the partial?"

I had to wait while he stubbed out a Tareyton and lit a fresh one from the smoldering butt.

"You're in luck, Harry," he said. "It's a stolen plate on a stolen car. Reported stolen yesterday evening from a druggist named Pete Quince in Bromley."

Bromley was a little town due west of Covington and Newport, about five miles downriver from Cincinnati.

"I don't suppose this Quince had any idea who stole his Caddie?" I asked.

"Why sure he did, Harry. He took after the thief on foot and got shot in the head."

I thought Al was kidding. But he wasn't.

"The guy who stole Quince's Cadillac also stole a

whole shitload of narcotics from Quince's drugstore, Saturday night about nine o'clock. Armed robbery and aggravated homicide. By the bye the Kentucky SP would very much like to know where you spotted this vehicle."

"I *didn't* spot it," I said. "A friend of mine was almost run down by it."

"When was this?"

"Late last night on River Road."

Al Foster stared at me morosely. "Why do I get the feeling you're not telling me the whole story?"

"Because I'm not."

Al sighed, breathing tusks of smoke out his hairy nostrils. Smoke seemed to cling to every part of him, like he'd been baptized in sulfur when he was a baby. "Aw, fuck it. What do I care? It's a Kentucky thing."

"I need another favor, Al."

Foster snorted so hard he blew the cigarette out of his mouth onto the desk. "God, you have balls," he said, snatching the butt up again.

"I want the LEADS sheet of a guy named Bob Adams."

"You do, do you? Any particular Bob Adams? FBI Quantico's probably got a couple thousand in the data banks."

"I can be a little more specific."

I gave him the description of Adams that Leon had given me and Pavel Fleischer had confirmed. "He may have been a Marine. At least he has a 'Semper Fi' tattoo on his arm. He worked as a singer in the seventies and rep'd for a record company sometime in the mid-to-late eighties. Also he's got a southern accent, maybe Kentucky or Tennessee."

"That'll narrow it down," Al said, scribbling down what I'd told him. "It'd be even better if you had prints."

"Well, I don't have prints. All I have is what I told you. This is real important, Al. If you could run it right away . . ."

"I'll run it, Harry. But if this guy Adams is the guy who killed the druggist and stole the Caddie I expect to hear. And I mean as soon as you do."

If Adams was the guy who'd killed druggist Pete Quince, Sheila Mozkowski was in even more trouble than I'd supposed. In the space of about five hours on Saturday night, Bob Adams had committed armed robbery, grand theft auto, aggravated homicide, assault with intent, and kidnapping. A man that desperate wasn't likely to waste a lot of time on ransom negotiations. If Sheila Mozkowski or Leon Tubin didn't fork over the thirty grand, my guess was he'd kill the woman. How Bob had sniffed out the thirty thousand and what, if anything, he had to do with it, I didn't know. But Leon knew. I was sure of that.

So I drove back through the cold dusk to Jewish Hospital, parked in the garage, and walked down the long hallway that ran from the garage through the main floor of the hospital to the Ridgeway wing. It was dinnertime so there was nobody to bump into when I got off the elevator at the twelfth floor. I went past the nurses' station to the end of the north wing hallway. To my surprise there was no one standing outside Leon's door—none of the usual audio crowd. It made better sense to me when I walked into the room.

Leon's bed was empty. Alas, so was Mr. Goldfarb's.

I went back up to the nurses' station and asked one of the candystripers which floor Leon had been transferred to.

"I think you better talk to the head nurse," the girl said with just enough alarm in her voice to make me nervous.

The head nurse, a barrel-shaped black woman wearing a name tag that read "T. Seeger," gave me a dark look.

"Leon Tubin left the hospital around an hour ago."

"He left?" I said with shock. "What do you mean he left?"

Head Nurse T. Seeger put her hands on her hips and stared at me down her nose. "Now what do you think I mean? He checked out of the hospital. We just treat 'em, mister. We can't keep 'em in a bed if they don't want to stay there."

"For chrissake."

"Don't you raise your voice," she snapped. "Don't you think we did everything we could to talk him out of it? That boy has a concussion, a dislocated jaw, a broken nose, cracked ribs, a bruise on his left kidney—and God knows how many contusions and lacerations. But he could walk and he could pay his bill at the bursar's office. And that's all it takes to get out of here."

"Exactly what happened when he left?" I asked.

"What do you mean 'what happened'? I just told you he walked out."

"I mean before he walked out. Did he get a phone call? Was there anyone in the room with him?"

"Ask Miss Reich here," Nurse Seeger said. "She was on duty."

The little candystriper slipped in front of the head nurse, like a kid coming out from behind her mother's skirt. "I went down to Mr. Tubin's room to check his dosage. There was another man in the room with him."

"Was he a big man, with red hair and a square face and blue eyes?"

The girl shook her head. "No. He was little. And he had a sharp sort of face. Foxy-looking."

It didn't sound like anyone I'd met. But it didn't sound like Bob Adams, either.

"As I was checking the glucose bottle, the phone rang. This other man answered it and handed the receiver to Mr. Tubin. Mr. Tubin listened for a while and turned kinda gray. He hung up the phone and told this other guy to help him out of bed—he was going home."

"He said he was going home?"

The girl nodded. "The other one helped him get dressed and took him down on the elevator.

"I tried to stop him," she said, tearing up. "But he just wouldn't listen."

If the call had been from whom I thought it was from, I could understand why Leon wouldn't listen. I turned on my heel and started for the elevators. Behind me I could hear Nurse Seeger soothing her friend.

"Don't you let that man upset you. You did your job just fine. It's not your fault that fool in 1222 was crazy. There are always going to be some crazy fools in this world."

# 14

**I MADE THE TRIP** to Leon's house in less than fifteen minutes, tearing out River Road to Saylor Park. From a block away I could see the lights in Leon's front windows. Lights all over the house.

I pulled up in the driveway, in front of a beat-up Subaru parked by the garage. Hopping out of the car, I ran up the steps to the front door, which was standing wide open, and through it into the barren living room. A short, fortyish man with a sharp-featured face and a spiky shock of brown hair was sitting on the sofa, reading a stereo magazine. The room around him had been turned upside-down. The speakers were lying on their sides. The TV was on the floor with its back torn off. The bottom plate of the amplifiers had been pried loose with a screwdriver. The preamplifier looked like it was broken in two pieces, and the turntable in three or four.

Even the cushions from the couch had been ransacked. Their covers were torn off and the pillows scattered on the floor, except for the one that the man with the stereo magazine was sitting on.

I glanced quickly at the dining room and saw the same shambles of broken and overturned furnishings.

"Leon?" the man on the couch said, turning a page of the magazine. "You got company."

I heard a groan in the dining room and saw Leon emerge from the darkness like Oedipus at Colonus.

The man on the couch glanced blithely over at him. "You O.K.? You need some help?" he said without moving a muscle.

Leon gave him a dirty look. "S'm h'lp," he said.

The little man hobbled into the living room, groaning with each step.

When he got to the living room he gave the guy on the couch a long look.

"You wanna sit down?" the man finally said.

He got up, still holding the magazine, as Leon literally collapsed on the single cushion. "O.K. if I take this to the john with me?" the guy asked. "There's a great article on Lyritas."

"Jus' go." Leon said, throwing his hand at him weakly.

The man walked out of the room, stepping through the debris as if it weren't there.

I stared at Leon.

"S'like s'n y'rslf in a m'r."

"Use a pad, will ya?"

Leon pointed to a pad and pencil sitting on the floor by a mangled stereo stand. I picked it up. Leon had already used it once, presumably with the guy from the couch, because there were a couple of words written on it in capital letters: "SHUT UP!"

I handed the pad to Leon, and he scribbled on it: "It's like seeing yourself in a mirror."

"You mean that guy?"

He nodded disgustedly. "Hank Diamond," he wrote. "Audiophile."

I looked around the room. "Was the house like this when you got here?"

Leon nodded again. "Fucking neighbors didn't hear a thing," he wrote on the pad.

It could've been the burglar or Adams. My guess was Adams. Sometime that afternoon he must've taken Sheila's key and broken into the house, searching for the thirty grand in the fridge. Only I'd already taken it to my office. It made me a little sick to think that Sheila might end up paying dearly for what I'd mistakenly done to protect her.

"What happened at the hospital?" I asked Leon.

"Got a call from 'Bob,'" he wrote. "Said he wanted the cash. Or he'd kill her. But I can't find the money!"

He looked up at me desperately.

"I've got it," I told him. "I put it in my office safe."

Leon started to cry. "Th'k G'd," he said, putting a shaking hand to his forehead.

I gave him a moment to collect himself. Somewhere in the back of the house I heard the john flush. A second later Hank Diamond walked back into the room.

"Hey, you O.K.?" he asked Leon, who was still weeping with a hand to his brow.

"He'll be fine," I said.

Hank Diamond gave me a casual once-over, as if he'd just noticed I was standing there. Which was probably the case. "Who are you, anyway?"

"Harry Stoner. I work for Leon."

"Yeah. What? Hi-fi repair?" Diamond glanced at the gutted stereo system. "He's gonna need some. Christ, you should see the basement."

It might have been my imagination—it was certainly unfair—but I thought I heard Leon sob even louder.

"He used to have a great record collection," Diamond said with relentless bad taste.

"Let's talk about it some other time."

Diamond shrugged. "Not talking about it isn't gonna change things. I lost my stereo once. Lightning hit my house."

That didn't surprise me.

"The insurance company called it an 'act of God.' "

I could only hope it was the first act on an ongoing smoting.

"Guess I'll go," Hank Diamond said, dropping the magazine at his feet. "S'long, Leon. Don't take any wooden records."

He went out the front door.

"Better move your car," he called over his shoulder. "Unless you want it to look like Leon's house."

I went out and moved the car. When I came back in Leon had fallen into a glassy-eyed torpor, as the enormity of what had befallen him and his settled over him.

"Ga' n'thn l'ff," he said in a leaden voice.

And he didn't. In the space of a day he'd lost almost

everything that mattered to him—his stereo, his records, and his faithless lover.

"We still have a chance to get Sheila back," I said without much confidence.

Swallowing hard Leon picked up the pad again. "Bob said he'd call me—here at the house," he wrote, "to arrange an exchange for the money."

"Did he let you talk to Sheila?"

Leon nodded. "She sounded scared," he wrote.

I could scarcely blame her. Bob Adams was a scary man.

"Where did all that money come from, Leon?" I asked.

He looked up at me and sighed. "She had it when we met," he wrote. "Said it was for a rainy day."

"It's raining, Leon."

He nodded grimly.

＝＝＝＝

I managed to pry a few more pieces of information about the money out of Leon Tubin, among which was the fact that Sheila had shown some of it to him on the first night that they'd made love, which, knowing Sheila, was probably the same day they met. Sheila was living in a dump in Anaheim at the time. She'd stored the cash in the refrigerator there, too, wrapped up in aluminum foil. Like the ones I'd opened, the brick she'd shown Leon was full of one-hundred-dollar bills. Sheila didn't tell him where she'd gotten all that cash. She just said it was insurance for a rainy day.

Over the years it had become a running joke with them—what they called the "freezer account." Sometimes Sheila talked about using the bread to make a comeback as a singer. Sometimes she talked about blowing it on a trip to Europe with Leon—making a grand tour of all the great orchestras and festivals. Sometimes, when she was pissed off, she said she was just going to take it and move out. But when it came down to it she never spent a dime of the freezer account.

Leon thought he knew why. "I looked inside one of the packages one afternoon," he wrote, scribbling laboriously on the dwindling pad of note paper. "The bills were in consecutive order, like they'd never been circulated. I think they might have come from something illegal."

"No shit, Leon," I said to him. "You sure she never mentioned this guy Bob Adams to you?"

"Never saw his face before," Leon wrote.

I knew through Pavel that Sheila had had an affair with Adams some years before. And since she was in the habit of confessing her past—and recent—indiscretions to Leon, I found it odd that the name Bob Adams had never come up.

I gave the little man a hard look. "Are you telling me the truth, Leon? I'm pretty sure Sheila and Adams . . . well, they were more than just friends at one time."

"You don't have to be polite," Leon scribbled, "Sheila has taken many lovers. I don't care."

"Why?" I asked.

"Because she loves me. You'll see."

I hoped that I would.

"Maybe he'll just take the money and go," he wrote in what appeared to be a slightly more hopeful hand.

"Maybe."

Only I wasn't counting on it. Bob Adams was simply too desperate to be trusted. He'd been burned once that afternoon, when Sheila had sent him to the house for the thirty grand. He was going to make very damn sure he got the bread the second time. I didn't think he cared what happened afterward.

That was when Leon dropped the bombshell.

"Most people would be happy with one hundred and seventy thousand dollars," he wrote.

"One hundred and seventy?" I said, feeling sick. "I only found three bricks in the freezer. Thirty thousand."

Leon dropped his pencil on the floor and stared at me with a stunned look on his face. "Wha' happ'n?"

"You got me," I said.

======

So we searched the house again. Leon and I. Mostly I.

Sifting through the rubble for aluminum foil, like a couple of bag ladies wheeling a shopping cart down Central Parkway. I knew when we started it was going to be a waste of time. I also knew that it had to be done, on the off-chance that Bob Adams had been so stoned on stolen pharmaceuticals that he'd overlooked one hundred and forty thousand bucks. I spent over two hours on my knees, peering under cabinets, inside the wreckage of closets, behind overturned desks and tipped-over dressers. I sifted through the twenty-three thousand records Bob Adams had dumped on Leon's basement floor. I checked the bathroom pipes like a plumber, the kitchen sink like a repairman—looking for a glint of aluminum or the gray-green corner of a hundred-dollar bill.

And I came up with nothing but a sore back and ruinous stains on the knees of my pants.

"Does Sheila have a legitimate bank account?" I asked Leon when, dusty and sweating, we'd finally given up the hunt. "Maybe some other hidey-hole in the house or the yard?"

Leon shook his head. A lively terror had begun to creep over him, making his eyes bug and his hands shake. He had reason to be scared. Bob Adams wasn't going to like being short-changed by one hundred and forty grand.

"I better talk to Al Foster at the CPD," I said, feeling some of the same terror creeping up my spine.

I picked up the phone, which was sitting on the floor by the couch—probably where Hank Diamond had left it, after charging a few long distance calls to Leon's number. As I started to dial, Leon lunged off the couch and tried to pull the receiver out of my hand.

"N'cop," he said hysterically.

I put a hand on his head and pushed him down gently on the sofa.

"Take it easy, for chrissake," I said. "I'm not going to tell him about Sheila."

He eyed me uncertainly. "Pro'ms?"

"I promise."

Folding his hands at his chest Leon sat back against the lone cushion and watched me nervously as I dialed the phone.

A desk sergeant answered. I asked him for Al Foster and got transferred to his extension. It was eight o'clock

by then, and there was a chance that Al had left for the
day—or for a fresh pack of Tareytons. But he was in.

"Tried to get you at your office," he said.

"I've been out."

"I ran the LEADS request and here's what I got.
You have a pencil?"

I grabbed the one Leon had dropped on the floor
and the pad he was holding.

"Bob Adams, a.k.a. Bobby Joe Bluenote, a.k.a Robert E. Lee Bernstein, a.k.a. Bobby Detroit."

"Bobby Detroit?"

"That was a stage name he used in '78," Al said.
"He sang and played piano with a group called Bobby
Detroit and the Motor City Music Lovers. They played
clubs in L.A. and Reno until Bobby was busted for the
sale and distribution of heroin in late '79. He did a two-
year rehab in Lexington. When he got out he started
another band, Robert E. Lee Bernstein and the Dixie
Crusaders."

"You're kidding."

"That's what it says," Al said. "He was arrested
again in '82 for armed robbery—a drugstore in Cleve-
land, Harry. The charge was dismissed because of some
Miranda shit. He was busted yet again in '83 in Akron—
same charge. This time he got shocked out after six
months—some court mix-up in his record. According to
the parole report he went back into the music biz briefly
in '85, before catching on as a rep with Atlantis Records
in '86. In '88 he had another band, called Bobby Joe
Bluenote's Southern Comfort. They were playing a two-
week stint across the river at the Quality Court motel in
Covington, when Adams was busted for possession of

heroin. This time he served a four-year stint in Lex, before being released on parole six and one half weeks ago. According to a report filed by his P.O. he was given permission to come to Cincinnati about three weeks ago, because of a job offer he'd received."

"What job offer?"

"We're trying to check that out. The P.O. isn't in on Sunday, so it might have to wait until tomorrow."

"Great," I said.

"You want to tell me what's going on, now?"

"I don't know what's going on."

"Sure," Foster said. "I'll read about it in the papers, right?"

"Al, give me a break. I'm telling you all I can."

I sounded like Leon, and the echo made me wince.

"Harry, this guy Adams is a long-time junkie who has a history of armed assault. He just got done murdering a man and he's on the run in a stolen car full of morphine ampoules. If you have reason to look him up, you sure as hell better let me know."

"I'll let you know," I told him.

He hung up the phone so hard it made my ear ring. I glanced at Leon, who was looking up at me with terror in his eyes.

"Did they find him?"

I shook my head. "We'll have to do it ourselves."

# 15

**AMONG OTHER THINGS** there was a good deal of newspaper scattered on Leon's floors. I managed to fish an entertainment page from Friday's *Post* out of the jumble.

"What's that for?" Leon wrote.

"I'm going to try to look for our boy and your girl," I told him.

It had occurred to me that Bob Adams had gone back into show business after each of his previous busts. I figured there was a good chance that he'd come to Cincinnati to do the same thing—to take a gig in a band or combo. It had also occurred to me that he knew that Sheila Mozkowski lived in Cincinnati or had been living there in '88. Which meant there was also a fair chance that the Cincy gig didn't exist—that it was simply a lie he'd told his P.O. in order to put himself within easy reach of Sheila and her hundred and seventy grand. If it had been a lie—and there were plenty of P.O.'s who would have bought the story without bothering to check it out—I didn't have a chance of finding Bob Adams. I had to hope that Adams's parole officer was the diligent type and that the job Bob had claimed to have taken here in town was legit.

I cleared a spot on the living room floor, spread the page out, and went through the weekend calendar listings of the performers playing in the greater Cincinnati area that weekend. I pored over every entry and every ad, looking for the names Bobby Detroit or Bobby Bluenote or Robert E. Lee Bernstein or Bobby Anybody. But I didn't find a headliner whose name was even remotely close to any of Adams's known aliases.

Then it dawned on me that if Adams *was* playing in a group, the chances of him headlining after four years in Lexington prison were pretty slim. It was more likely that he'd be playing backup for some small combo. What I needed to do was talk to a musician who knew the local music scene from the front row to the drum kit.

It was Sunday so calling the local branch of the musicians' union was out. I'd had a friend named Pete Ruggles, who played piano in a jazz combo at the Blue Wisp, but he'd moved on to New York. However, thinking of the Blue Wisp brought someone else to mind.

I turned to Leon, who was sitting stunned and silent on the couch—the pad and pencil lying in his lap. "Do you know a horn player named Philo Ives?"

Leon picked up the pencil. "Stereophile," he wrote. "Friend of LeRoy's."

Philo had looked like a flake to me, but when I

asked Leon what he thought of him he wrote: "He's a street guy. Not too crazy about honkies. But I like him. He's a real good musician."

"You think LeRoy would have his number?" I asked.

Leon nodded, yes.

Picking up the phone I dialed LeRoy Anderson's house.

"You know that damn Leon went and left Jewish Hospital?" LeRoy said, after I'd said hello.

"I'm sitting next to him right now," I told him.

"Where's that?"

"At his house in Saylor Park."

LeRoy made a tsking noise. "That boy is short on Schlitz. He should be in a hospital bed."

"He needs to be here, LeRoy," I said. "And I need a couple of favors from you."

"Go ahead and tell me what you need," LeRoy said, as if whatever I wanted was as good as done.

"First I'd like to talk to that musician friend of yours, Philo Ives."

LeRoy chuckled. "I'll see what I can do, Harry, but I don't think Philo much cottoned to you. What else you need?"

"This is asking a lot because it could be dangerous, but I'd like you to come over here and stay with Leon while I talk to Ives."

He didn't even hesitate. "I'm on my way."

While I was talking to LeRoy, Leon had been looking over the notes I'd taken of my conversation with Al Foster. As soon as I hung up he said, "Mus' L'rs," and pointed to the words "Bobby Detroit and the Motor City Music Lovers" on the notepad.

I nodded. "That's probably how Adams first met Sheila, when she was playing backup for his act in '78."

It was obvious that the Music Lovers had slid a long way downhill since they'd first come to L.A. in '72. By '78, when they'd joined up with Bobby Detroit, I figured that Sheila Mozkowski might have grown hard enough and desperate enough to do anything for a buck—including grand theft. Maybe with Bobby Adams-Bernstein-Bluenote-Detroit as her partner. It would explain how Adams had known about the money she was holding. It would also explain what Sheila meant when she talked about the bad company she was keeping before Leon saved her from disaster.

I didn't mention it to Leon but there was another item on the note sheet that was even more interesting than the one about the Music Lovers: the bust in '88 at the Quality Court motel, where Pavel Fleischer had gone to buy records from Adams and discovered Sheila Mozkowski in the room. I was thinking it was a damn convenient little bust—from Sheila's point of view.

I couldn't imagine that Adams had been any less greedy for money in '88 than he was in '92. In fact if I was right about him having a stake in the dough, he'd probably been hunting for Sheila Mozkowski for quite some time before he finally caught up with her in that Covington motel room. Luckily for Sheila, Adams was practically busted on the spot and shipped away to Lexington for four long years. The timing might have been the work of fate—Adams was a recidivist who was bound to end up in prison on his own hook sooner or later.

But in this instance I couldn't help wondering whether fate had been given a nudge.

If Bob Adams *had* been set up by Sheila Mozkowski in 1988, I couldn't see him letting her walk away from the kidnapping. Even if he did get the entire one-hundred-and-seventy-grand ransom, he'd want to pay her back for those four years in prison—not to mention the years he'd spent looking for her. It made it that much more imperative to find the son-of-a-bitch as quickly as possible.

LeRoy Anderson arrived at Leon's house around nine-thirty. I saw him pull up through the living room window. There was someone else sitting in the car with him. I thought it might be Philo Ives until the guy got out and stretched in the street light, all six feet eight of him. Sherwood Loeffler.

Leon couldn't see Loeffler from the couch—which was probably a good thing.

I watched LeRoy come up the front stairs to the stoop.

"What in the world happened here?" he said as he came through the door.

I said, "The guy that snatched Sheila paid Leon's house a visit."

"What the hell was he looking for—termites?"

LeRoy spotted the overturned stereo and clutched at his heart. "Oh, my Lord." He actually staggered for a moment.

"The bastard trashed Leon's system," he said as if a man could do no worse to another man.

But I knew better. "He may try to trash Leon. And you, too. The guy who did this is a desperate character, LeRoy, very crazy and very dangerous."

"You figurin' he might come back here?" he asked.

"It's possible."

I described Bobby Adams to LeRoy, then told him to call the police if Adams showed up at the door. However LeRoy had his own plan of defense.

"I'll blow the motherfucker's nuts off," he said, pulling a long-barreled .44 Ruger out of his coat.

"Just don't blow your own nuts off," I said. "And under no circumstances are you to leave this house until I get back. Either of you."

I gave Leon a pointed look.

"Now about Philo?" I asked LeRoy.

The old man raised a hand. "That's all taken care of."

Grabbing my coat sleeve he pulled me away from the couch, out of Leon's earshot.

"I called Philo after you called me," he whispered. "He didn't much want to talk to you, just like I thought. He don't like strangers. Especially white ones. But he does know that tall drink of water outside there. And halfway trusts him. So I drug him along."

"Sherwood knows Philo?" I said with surprise.

Leon started just a bit on the sofa. "Sher'd?"

"Keep your voice down, Harry," LeRoy whispered. "You gonna give Leon a heart attack. Sure, Sherwood knows Philo. He's been to Philo's house a coupla times."

"To his house?"

LeRoy grinned. "Philo's a stereophile, Harry. And a new system's better'n a steak dinner to Sherwood. He just cain't wait to dig in and start cutting. Anyway that big, tall ass may come in handy. Large as he is he scares most people just from looking at him. And the way Philo acts sometimes, you might need to do some scaring."

I felt a little miffed that LeRoy Anderson hadn't thought I was smart enough or tough enough to tackle Philo Ives on my own. But then I hadn't been doing a particularly impressive job of detecting up till then. And when it came down to it I didn't think LeRoy had much faith in the native wit of white people, especially non-stereophile white people.

I told Leon I'd be back as soon as I could manage, and he said something indecipherable, which I took to be a plea to rescue Sheila. As I walked out the door LeRoy Anderson shut and locked it behind me.

Out on the street Loeffler was pacing the sidewalk like a beat cop.

"Hey, there, Har'," he said in, what was for him, a moderated boom.

"Sherwood," I said, shaking my head. "What the hell are you doing here?"

"Why, didn't LeRoy tell ya?" he said, drawing himself up to his full six eight. "I speak fluent Negro."

———

Philo Ives lived in English Woods, a rent-controlled housing project at the top of Fairmount hill. It was a notoriously dangerous place for residents and visitors alike, although Sherwood Loeffler didn't seem to be daunted.

"Now don't get your hopes up," he said as I pulled onto the drive that wound through the rundown brick apartment houses, "we aren't likely to see any shootings tonight. Sundays are a day of rest among the colored peoples."

"Can it, will you, Sherwood? It isn't funny."

"Certainly, Har'." He pointed to a street on the left. "Turn down here."

I followed his finger down a short side street. Philo's apartment building was at the end of the block, just another four-unit brick hut set in another dark, treeless plot. There was a Ford Fairlane parked in front of it, tricked out with gold-rimmed hubcaps, a tuxedo trunk, sidelights, and a beaver tail on the cellular phone antenna.

"Makes you want to buy American, don't it?" Sherwood said.

I parked behind the Fairlane and we got out into the cold night air.

"As I recall Philo's on the first floor, to the right. Course I could be wrong. Last time I was here he had the blinds open and you could see that saxophone on the rug."

Philo did have a sax on his living room rug—a tenor sax sparkling on a stand between two columnar loudspeakers. There were also a couple of playbills on the walls, with his name prominently displayed as featured performer. It gave me hope that he could help out with Adams.

Ives was dressed for bed when he answered the door—a long black robe cinched loosely at his waist by a belt with a pager hanging from it. Without the sunglasses on he was a good-looking guy, mid-thirties, surprisingly muscular, with a nervous, street-smart,

coal-black face. Most of the musicians I had known—
black and white—were fairly laid-back men, with personalities that suited their instruments. This guy was
wired so tight he could have played bedsprings.

Running a hand over his fade, Philo scowled at me.
His expression softened a little when he saw Sherwood
looming in the hall. At that point I was beginning to
think that it probably had been a good idea to bring
Loeffler along. But the night was young yet.

"Hey, homes," Ives said to Sherwood. He didn't say
anything to me.

Sherwood pushed past me into the living room.

"How's the system, Philo?"

Philo shook his head. "Almost blew a woofer last
night. It's that damn amp LeRoy sold me. That old man
done cheated me for the last time."

"You sure you weren't playing a tad too loud?"
Sherwood said, settling on a sofa across from the stereo
rig. "You folks do tend to play your music rather
loudly."

Philo shook his head as if he'd been down this particular road before with Sherwood. It amazed me that
people seemed to put up as well as they did with Sherwood Loeffler's shenanigans.

"My folks, huh?" Philo said disgustedly. "At least I
*can* play loud."

Sherwood flushed as if Philo had insulted *his* race—
the race of electrostats. "My speakers will play every bit
as loudly as these paper-coned numbers," he said with
umbrage. "Besides the kind of music I listen to isn't
meant for a boom box."

"And Miles is, huh?"

"Miles who? Is he some sort of musician?"

Philo stared at him icily. "Keep it up, Sherwood, and I'm gonna get my jammie out."

Sherwood grinned. "Just pulling your leg, Philo, old boy."

"I'm gonna *cut* your leg," Philo said under his breath, "if you call me boy one more time." He looked at me—hard. "As long as it's white night, I guess you can come in, too. We ain't giving away no detergent or dishes, though."

I went into the living room and sat down on the couch beside Sherwood. The furniture was hi-tech leather. The lamps were halogen. The carpet an expensive Persian number. If it all came from music Philo Ives had done very well for himself.

Ives gave me a sidelong glance before walking over to a slung leather chair. He really must not have cottoned to me, because he kept staring coldly at me as he sat down.

"How 'bout some music?" Sherwood boomed, rubbing his hands together vigorously.

It occurred to me that LeRoy had been right—around stereo systems he really did act like he was sitting down to a steak dinner.

"What do you want to hear?" Philo asked, perking up a little.

"Whatever you got on the 'table."

"I got some 'Trane on the 'table."

"Put it on, put it on."

Philo walked over to the turntable—a monstrous contraption sitting on four small pillars.

Leaning over to Loeffler I said, "This isn't a stereo night, Sherwood."

"Jus' softening him up," he said with a grin.

John Coltrane came on—loudly.

Philo's speakers seemed to inch across the floor, driven by the rhythm of the horns. They were, indeed, loud and they had a quality of presence I hadn't heard in any of the other music lovers' systems, although under the circumstances it annoyed me that I was hearing differences at all. Sherwood Loeffler was what my mother would have called a bad influence.

"Great!" Sherwood boomed, tapping his foot and pounding a palm on his knee.

"You're off the beat there, Sherwood," Philo said dryly.

"I'm just gettin' the hang of it. This stuff's got a certain animal drive I hadn't never noticed before. Must be your system, Phi."

Philo shook his head. He obviously had too much street smarts to buy anybody's line of bull, especially the blatant crap that Sherwood Loeffler was doling out. And to a professional jazz musician—and a pretty good one judging from the posters—Sherwood's condescension must have been, in Larry Peacock's memorable phrase, intolerable. But in spite of all that, Philo was a stereophile. And that meant that a choice bit of his ego was vulnerable to just the kind of woo that Sherwood was pitching. The way to a stereophile's heart is through his system. It was a lesson that Sherwood knew, too.

"You like the sound, huh?" Philo said.

"Couldn't be better," Sherwood told him.

Philo Ives smiled. "You white boys want some bread and marmalade or something?"

Sherwood chuckled. "We'll pass on the refreshments, Philo, although I think my friend here might want to ask you a few innocent questions."

"Yeah?" Philo looked me up and down. "What kinda innocent questions?"

"I'm looking for a musician named Bob Adams," I told him. "A white guy in his forties, used to go under the name Bobby Detroit and Bobby Bluenote and Bob Bernstein. I have reason to believe that he may be playing in town right now."

"What's this honky look like?" Philo asked.

I gave him a description of Adams, down to the tattoo.

"Does the dude blow horn?"

"Maybe. I know he sings and plays the piano."

"Rocket Club," Philo said.

Before I could ask him what "Rocket Club" meant, his pager went off.

"You gents'll excuse me," he said, getting up from the chair and walking down a hall into a back room.

"You ever heard of a Rocket Club?" I asked Sherwood.

"Cain't say that I have. You think it's an aeronautical society, mebbe?"

Standing up, Sherwood walked over to Philo's record cabinet and started thumbing through the LP's as if he were thumbing through the man's checkbook stubs. "Let's see what old Philo's got good."

I glanced down the hall. Philo had gone into what

looked like a bedroom, shutting the door behind him. I heard him laugh loudly, then I heard Sherwood whistle.

"Now I *will* be damned," he said.

I looked back at Loeffler. He was standing by the record cabinet, holding a beat-up record in his hands.

I heard Philo open the bedroom door. So did Sherwood. He tucked the record on the shelf and scurried back to the couch, sitting down just as Philo came into the room.

"Just a little business," Ives said jovially. "Now, y'all wanted to know about some honky named Joe Smith or Bob Adams?"

I nodded.

"Well I don't know about that Adams groove, but there's a white boy plays piano been filling in down at the Rocket last week or so. He looks a lot like the dude you're talking about. Only he calls himself Ross Finley."

"Where is this Rocket Club?"

"Mohawk," Philo said, passing a hand along the top of his fade. "Rocket Club Number Two."

"Where is number one?" Sherwood asked.

"Right under Number Two. Burned down 'bout two years ago and they built the new one on the same spot."

"Rather like the various walls of Troy," Sherwood said.

"Now y'all gonna have to excuse me, 'cause I got company coming."

We both stood up.

"I'll get in touch, Philo," Sherwood said. "Talk records, maybe?"

"You already screwed me out of too many records, Sherwood. You and that shylock Leon."

"Now, Philo," Sherwood said. "We mustn't call other people names."

# 16

**SHERWOOD SEEMED** altogether too pleased with himself when we got back out to the Pinto. I figured it had something to do with the record he'd found in Philo's cabinet. Judging from what Ives had said, Sherwood and Leon had been skimming records from Philo's collection for some years.

"What're you grinning about?" I said, unlocking the car doors.

"Just a private joke, Harry. I found me a little nugget of gold in Philo's record collection."

"You gonna try to trade him for it?"

"Been cutting KFC coupons for a month."

"I don't think it's gonna work, Sherwood."

But he was still smiling as he eased himself onto the passenger seat. "You'd be surprised, Harry, how easy it is to prey on the suspicious, untutored mind."

I dropped Loeffler off at his house on Fairfield, then turned around and drove back down to Gilbert, cutting over Reading to Liberty and then a few blocks up the Parkway to the tumble-down neighborhood called Over-the-Rhine. It was called Over-the-Rhine because until the turn of the century it had been a German immigrant neighborhood with a canal running through it. The only things running through it anymore were cops chasing crack heads and arsonists. The narrow, twisty streets were lined with dilapidated brownstones, many of them burned out or boarded up. Even the doors to the Gayety Theater, a magnet of my youth, were now boarded over, although the billboard marquee still promised "Brand-New Girls—Every Week." Old men in trench coats, college kids in heat, Appalachian girls just up from West Virginia willing to strip down to a G-string for minimum wage—ah, youth!

The Rocket Club Number Two was a block down from the Gayety, on the south side of the windswept corner between the Parkway and Mohawk Avenue. The place didn't look like it had been built on the ruins of another club—it looked like the ruins themselves. There was a splintered neon sign on the wall, bars on the windows, holes in the brick, a couple of drunks in overcoats teetering like saw-cut timber on either side of the door, and the faint, triumphal note of a trumpet cutting through the wreckage—like the dedication of a building in hell.

I parked across from the Rocket Club on Mohawk, locked the Pinto tight, and scurried to the other side of the windy street, past the tottering drunks and through the Rocket's front door.

There was a leather-railed bar just inside the door, running halfway down the room. Beyond it the walls bellied out into a small dance floor, surrounded by half-empty linoleum tables. At the back of the dance floor a step-up bandstand was lit harshly by spots. Everything else in the place was dark, save for the lighted tips of cigarettes and the occasional flash of eyes. The club smelled like cigarettes and booze and the rotten meat smell of rat poison. As far as I could tell I was the only other honky in the joint—me and Ross Finley a.k.a. Bobby Adams.

I didn't see Mr. Finley on the stage. In fact I didn't see anyone on the stage. The trumpet I had heard on the street was playing on a jukebox.

I sat down at the first stool by the rail. A black bartender with a white shirt, a bow tie and a shiny, knobby face, puckered like a cleft chin at the brow, came over to take my order.

"Draft," I said, pulling a couple of bills out of my pants and laying them on the bar.

He tapped a glass and put it down in front of me.

"When's the next set?" I asked him.

"You're hearing it right now."

"I thought you had a live show," I said with surprise. "A friend of mine, Ross Finley, told me he'd be playing piano here tonight."

"Uh-huh. Well your friend quit last week."

"He get another gig?"

"I doubt it," the guy said without explaining.

I got the impression Ross had been a lot of trouble. Junkie ex-cons have a tendency that way.

I said, "You don't happen to know where he went, do you?"

"Don't know and don't care." The bartender scooped the money up and moved off up the bar.

The guy sitting next to me, an old black man with an alcoholic's shaky hands and pouchy, haggard face, tried out a broken-toothed smile before cadging a drink.

"You like jazz, huh?" he said in a hoarse voice.

"Yeah," I said, but I was thinking about what to do next. And not coming up with anything bright.

"That Finley could play some—for a white boy. Had him that strong left hand like Tatum."

"Yeah, he's one of the greats."

I got up from the bar stool, and the old man tugged at my coat sleeve.

"Thought you wanted to know where he was," he said bluntly.

I sat down again—smiling. "That's right, pop. You know where Finley is?"

"I know somebody who does."

I took a twenty out of my wallet and hailed the bartender. "Give my friend here a . . ."

"Rye," the old man said. "Rye's always been good enough for me."

The bartender poured him a tumbler from a silver-spouted bottle, shot me a contemptuous look—as if he thought I was taking advantage of the old drunk—and went back up the rail.

"My name's Samuel Bass," the old man said. "You can call me Sammy."

"Harry Stoner," I said, shaking his fingertips,

which was the only part of his hand he offered. "Who's this friend you were talking about, Sammy?"

"Ellen Cagney. She's just up the bar a ways. She and that white boy were pretty close for a week or two, till he give her a black eye and kicked her ass."

She sounded like my kind of witness—hostile to Bobby.

I picked up my beer glass and grabbed Sammy Bass by the arm. "Let's go talk to her."

Sammy Bass took his drink in one hand and collected the change from the twenty with his other, sliding it over to the rail and into the pocket of his overcoat.

"Well, then," he said, and started up the bar.

A spruce young black woman with a mouse around her right eye and a split lower lip was sitting at one of the tables near the bandstand. A couple of tough-looking men in leather sports jackets were sitting on either side of her. All three of them were in their cups and laughing like crazy. They laughed even harder when Sammy and I walked up.

"Is the circus in town?" the woman said with a hoot.

"Ellen, this man here's a friend of Ross Finley's," Sammy said.

The woman stopped laughing immediately and, a second later, so did her two tough-looking companions.

At that moment I wished that Sammy Bass had let me make my own introductions.

"I'm not exactly a friend of his," I said to Ellen Cagney, who was staring at me like I was wearing a Ross Finley look-alike mask.

"You better not be his friend," the woman said icily.

"Hey, babe?" one of the men said, looking me up

and down. He was packed into the leather sports coat like a blood sausage. "This guy bothering you?"

"He's fixing to. What is it you want from me, mister?"

I decided it was time to shift identities.

"I want you to tell me how to find Finley," I said sharply. "The son-of-a-bitch owes me money. That's why I came to this dump looking for him. I heard he was playing piano here."

"Well, he ain't playing piano here anymore."

She said it like she'd fired him personally. Which was possible. The guys on either side of her were big enough to be bouncers, and they were kowtowing to her like she ran the place.

"You don't know where he went, do you?" I asked.

The woman thought it over for a second. "You gonna have him arrested?"

"I'm gonna shoot him," I said with a wink.

"That's good." Ellen Cagney laughed and, a second later, the two guys started laughing with her.

"He's gonna fatten up his ass," the big-shouldered guy said to the other one.

"I can't tell you where he is right this moment," the woman said. "But the last time I saw the no-good son-of-a-bitch he was standing in a room in the Lincoln Hotel, and I was lying on the floor right under his feet."

"The Lincoln on Main Street?"

"Yeah. One week he's in the Lincoln begging me for a job. The next he's got cash in his pants and I got me a two-hundred-dollar Emergency Room bill. You find him, you shoot him again for me."

I told her I would.

The Lincoln Hotel was a rattrap on Main Street near Sixth—the sort of welfare dump that only a down-and-outer would stay in. And so Ross Finley a.k.a. Bobby Adams had been, according to Ellen Cagney. At least he'd been that way for a week or so, and then he'd suddenly gotten well. Maybe he'd robbed a liquor store or another pharmacy. I had all sorts of notions about where he might have found some loose change.

It was past eleven according to my watch on a Sunday night in January. So there was absolutely no one but me on Sixth Street when I pulled up across from the Lincoln. I parked in a Parkade next to Izzy's and sat in the car, under the queer yellow sodium vapor lights of the lot, and stared at the grimy facade of the hotel. It was as dead-end a place as you could find in this town—a five-story flop, full of rootless, desperate men.

I keep a .38 Airweight inside the glove compartment—for those few occasions when I find myself sitting across from dead-end hotels. I pulled the piece out of the glove box, tucked it in my coat, then got out of the car and walked across Main to the Lincoln.

Inside the front door of the Lincoln Hotel a narrow hall—half battered wainscoting, half peeling plaster—led past a bus terminal bench to the caged-in desk of the night clerk. There were pictures of Jesus up and down the peeling walls. Jesus in the Manger, Jesus in the Temple, Jesus on the Mount, Jesus on the Cross, Jesus Appearing to Mary Magdalene. The only picture they didn't have hanging on the wall was the only one that was appropriate—Jesus Harrowing Hell.

An old man in two or three layers of ratty cardigan sweaters was sleeping on the bench opposite the caged-in desk. His mouth was hanging open and a long trail of saliva hung like a spiderweb between his lip and the lapel of his sweater. Another man, just barely awake himself, sat in the lighted booth behind the desk. He was a stout man, wearing an overcoat and an earmuff hat.

"Kin I do for you?" he said listlessly.

A small portable TV was going on his desk, and he had a hard time taking his eyes off it.

"I want to see Ross Finley," I said, banging on the cage to get his attention.

The guy looked up, startled. "He ain't in."

"How do you know that?"

" 'Cause he ain't been in for a week. Paid for three weeks, only stayed here two." The guy looked me over. "I could let you see his room if you're wanting to stay—$17.50, in advance."

It was a neat system of double-bookkeeping—and an easy $17.50 for the clerk, who knew as well as I did that I had no intention of staying the night. He had me pegged for a private cop—I could see it in his eyes. Of course in that joint he'd had plenty of experience with the law.

I gave the guy a twenty and he gave me a key.

"Number 42." He jerked his thumb toward an open elevator beside the cage. "Fourth floor, front."

I got in the elevator, which was barely big enough for one of me, and pressed four.

The thing lurched upward with a rattle of chains. As it crept up to four I read some of the graffiti on the walls. Women's names. Slogans like Born to Lose, Mother, Jesus Wept. Faraway towns. It was like a tattoo parlor, only they'd scratched the words on the walls. Generations of them.

The elevator lurched and rattled again when it stopped at four. The door slid open on a dim hallway, lined like the lobby with accordion-wainscoting and lighted by thirty-watt bulbs, strung like Christmas lights from a dangling overhead wire. The hallway smelled of dry rot and sour beer and the greasy, canned foods that the tenants heated up on their two-burner stoves. I walked down to the front of the building. Number 42 was at the far end of the hall, to the right of a pair of grimy casement windows, looking out on Main Street. The hotel room door was painted black, with the number "42" stenciled on it in white letters. I unlocked the door with the key the clerk had given me and went inside.

I could see an unmade bed in one corner of the room, lit by the moonlight crawling through the dirty front window. There was a chifforobe at the head of the bed—painted over so many times it almost looked enameled. Its open door was hanging from one hinge. From where I was standing there didn't look to be anything on the dark shelves inside it.

I fumbled along the wall, looking for a light switch. And when I couldn't find one, I went over to the bed and clicked on a small lamp just above the headboard. It was a fifteen-watt bulb, hardly better than a candle, but in the faint light I could see that the chifforobe was, indeed, empty. I went through the rest of the room—

the little there was of it—and didn't find a thing. No clothing, no suitcase, no magazine, no pack of matches.

Bob Adams had left in the night, and hadn't left a thing behind him. Just like he'd seen me coming.

The guy who *had* seen me coming was still sitting behind the caged-in desk when I stepped back off the elevator on the ground floor. I rattled his cage again, and he looked up wide-eyed.

"You could've told me Finley moved out."

"I did tell you," the man said nervously. "I haven't seen him in a week."

"Did Finley have any visitors while he was here?" I asked him.

When he didn't say anything I took another twenty out of my wallet and slapped it on the counter. The guy in the earmuffs snapped it up like a frog spearing a fly.

"Some black broad used to visit him," he said, rolling the twenty up like cigarette paper and sticking it behind his earmuff. "Fact, they had a helluva row right before he moved out."

"He didn't leave a forwarding address, did he? Or a telephone number?"

The man in the earmuffs laughed. "Yeah, he left an engraved card. All our guests do."

"How 'bout messages. Did he get any messages?"

The guy began squeezing his dick as if he had to pee.

"He had a few. Some other broad called him after he moved out—looking to fuck him, I guess. That's what it sounded like, anyway. You know, I'm waiting for him in bed kind of thing. I left messages in his box, but he never come back to pick them up." He started shifting feet. "I gotta piss, so let's make this quick."

"Do you recall the woman's name?"

He shook his head and squeezed his dick a little tighter.

"It wasn't Sheila Mozkowski, was it?"

If I'd thought about it I wouldn't have bothered asking. Sheila would scarcely have called Bob Adams up. In fact she would have done her damnedest to stay as far away from the man as possible. But her name was the only one that came to mind—the only woman in town, outside of Ellen Cagney, who I knew for a fact had screwed Bobby Detroit.

So I said it, and nearly grabbed my own crotch when the clerk with the earmuffs said, "Yeah. I think that was the name."

"You're kidding," I said, stunned.

"I don't kid cops."

"You still have the messages?"

"Kept 'em for a week, then tossed 'em out." He unlocked the cage door and stepped out from behind the desk. "I gotta go."

"Frank!" he shouted to the old man sleeping on the bench.

Frank stirred himself slowly. Half a pint of fluid dripped out of his mouth when he sat up.

"I gotta take a leak," the proprietor said to him. "Watch the desk."

Frank waved a hand at him listlessly and cleaned his mouth up with the sleeve of his cardigan.

"That guy used to be a semipro ballplayer in the

forties," the guy with the muffs said. "Well, I guess we all used to be something."

He walked quickly up the hall with the pictures of Jesus on them to a door marked "Office" and disappeared behind it.

# 17

SOMETHING WAS DEFINITELY WRONG with the picture of
Sheila Mozkowski the desk clerk had painted, and I
didn't know whether to ask Leon about it or not. He'd
taken a bad beating and spent a day and a night worry-
ing himself sick about the woman. I didn't want to be
the one to tell him that his girlfriend had been screwing
the guy who kidnapped her—again.

That was the way it looked, though, if the clerk had
been right about the telephone messages. The Lincoln
Hotel message didn't necessarily mean that the kidnapping itself was queer. I didn't think there was enough
money on earth to make Sheila voluntarily put Leon in
for the kind of a beating he took. But I'd been wrong
about people before, especially when big money was involved. And money was at the heart of the case—I was
convinced of that. Ellen Cagney had told me that Finley/

164

Adams had found a whole bunch of cash overnight. And short of armed robbery the only place he could have gotten it was Sheila. Maybe she'd broken into one of those missing aluminum bricks.

When I thought it over, it made some sense that she would try to pay Adams off—with her body or her dough or both. A guy looks her up after being in prison for four years—a junkie, a thief, a thoroughly bad man. This guy is definitely pissed off, probably suspects that Sheila set him up for his last bust, and isn't going to take no for an answer to any question. What do you do with a guy like that?

You make him happy and try to get rid of him. Just as she'd done in '88.

Apparently, screwing him and feeding him a few bucks didn't do the trick this time. And she hadn't had the time to set Adams up for another bust. Old Bob hadn't given her the time. But I had an inkling of what she might have been up to—and a guess as to why one hundred and forty thousand dollars was missing from the freezer fund. It occurred to me that Sheila might have split the boodle up once she'd found that Bob was back on her trail—hiding the big half and hoping to con Adams into thinking that the remaining thirty grand was all she had left after thirteen years on the run. Only Adams hadn't given her the chance to buy him off cheaply. Sheila's luck had run out on Saturday night, and whatever game she'd been playing with Bob had presumably ended there.

I decided to keep my speculation to myself until I had a better fix on who had been conning whom. But I couldn't avoid calling Leon's house—I had to know if Adams had phoned for ransom.

I found a booth across from the Lincoln on the corner of Sixth and dialed Leon's number. LeRoy answered on the second ring.

"Had any visitors?" I asked him, after saying hello.

"Been quiet as a well-kept grave," LeRoy said sleepily. "Nobody come by and nobody called 'cept Sherwood."

"What did he want?"

"He said he had to talk to you," LeRoy said.

"About what?"

"Something about Sheila he said you had to know. Told me to tell you to come by his house anytime up till 2 A.M. He made it sound real important, Harry."

Sherwood Loeffler had a strong streak of amateur detective in him.

"O.K.," I said. "I'll give him a buzz."

I glanced at my watch, which was showing half-past eleven. "Ask Leon something for me?"

"Why sure," LeRoy said. "May take a little while to get the answer. I gotta wait for him to write it out."

"Ask him whether Sheila had been acting like herself this last week or two?"

I heard LeRoy repeat the question to Leon.

A few moments later, LeRoy came back on the line, chuckling. "He said she was a little bitchier than usual. He said you should know that better than most."

Leon had a point. That first night I'd come to his house Sheila had put on quite a show—drunk, licentious, cranky, not giving a damn about Leon or anyone else. The following afternoon she'd been a different and far more likable woman—smart, brassy, semiresponsible.

"Ask Leon if Sheila had been spending more time out of the house last week than she does normally?" I said to LeRoy.

There was another long pause.

"Leon says she went out a few times last week and was gone for a coupla hours each time. He doesn't know where she went. He also wants to know why you're asking these questions."

"Tell him I'm just being nosy," I said to LeRoy. "I'll call back in a few hours. Meantime, both of you stay alert."

"Will do," he said, hanging up.

I dug another quarter out of my pocket and dialed Nick Charles.

"Harry, you gotta come out here," Sherwood said in an excited voice.

"Sherwood, this is no time to be fucking around."

"I ain't fucking around," he said obstinately. "You just come out here and judge for yourself. I'll leave a light on for you."

"All right," I said, "but it better be good."

=====

It was a quarter of twelve when I pulled up in front of Sherwood Loeffler's picture-book house. As promised the front porch light was on. I walked up the snowy walk to the stoop and knocked. Sherwood answered a moment later, as if he'd been waiting breathlessly on the other side of the door. Maybe it was the late hour but he looked weirder than usual. His face was aglow with excitement, as if he'd just got done *shtupping* his wife—or his neighbor.

"Man," he boomed, "I didn't think you'd get the message."

"I got it. But I'm gonna have to make this quick. No music, Sherwood. We're coming down to the wire now—and Sheila's standing on it."

Sherwood rubbed his hands together ominously. "Harry, my boy, come into my parlor."

I followed him into the sitting room that Leon had tried to set afire the day before. Sherwood walked directly into the anteroom and came back holding a record. I could see the lamplight playing on its polished surface.

My blood pressure shot up so high my face turned red. "You brought me out here to show me a record!"

"Ah, but this isn't just any ol' record. This is a genuine, 10/s, Indianapolis-pressed, shaded dog LSC-1817."

"So?"

Sherwood's long face fell like someone had hooked a barbell to his jaw. Gape-mouthed he stared at me disbelievingly. "Don't you git it?"

"I'm afraid I don't."

"This is *Gaîté Parisienne,* Harry. Arthur Fiedler? The Boston Pops?"

I stared at him blankly.

One of Sherwood's eyes started to float disturbingly around his face. "Jesus, you are a dunce! This is *Leon's* record!"

This time *my* jaw dropped. "Leon's record. Where the hell did you get it?"

"From Philo. This is the record I found on his shelf

earlier tonight." Sherwood's face lit up with cunning and exaltation. "Now ain't you gonna ask me where Philo got it?"

"You know the answer?"

He nodded and, raising his hand like a conductor at the start of a piece, brought it down in a crashing downbeat. "He stole it from Leon's house."

"You telling me that Philo was the thief!" I said with astonishment.

Sherwood nodded. "And you know who gave him a key to git in that house and told him exactly which records to take?"

Feeling like a schoolboy at a kiddie concert I shook my head, no.

Sherwood brought his hand down again with finality. "Little Miss Sheila."

Sherwood tried to explain it to me as we raced over to Philo's hut in English Woods.

"I knew it was Leon's record soon as I saw it. But I didn't let on." He chuckled. "I was just storing up my ammunition—planning to give Philo both barrels soon as I called him up. Which is what I did the minute after you dropped me off. Oh, he tried to weasel his way out of it. Your lower-class black will do just about anything to shirk responsibility."

"Jesus," I said under my breath.

"But I had him and he knew it. Hell, I wrote the damn serial number down when I spotted the record at the library sale—before that ki— before poor Leon took it off my pile."

He was enjoying himself. And maybe he had a right to crow.

"I told Philo, real sadlike, that if he didn't bring that record straight over to my house I'd just have to call the police—what with my little pal's wife being abducted and kidnapping being such a serious charge. I believe it carries the death penalty in this state, don't it?"

Sherwood snapped an imaginary baton between his clenched fists. "He broke like a bread stick and brought the thing right over. I hated to do it. I hate to strip a man of his self-respect and pride."

"Especially a black man."

"Honor knows not color or creed, Harry. I did this for poor Leon."

Uh-huh, I said to myself. "You blackmailed Philo, Sherwood."

"That's a harsh term for an act of daring that may help you—how do they put this on TV—crack the case? Of course I expect to retain the record as a reward."

"It's Leon's record."

"Not no more it ain't," he said firmly.

"Did Philo tell you why Sheila hired him to steal Leon's records?"

"Now, that's a touchy subject," Sherwood said. "I think it's best that you and Philo take it up separately."

I was going to take it up with him all right. The son-of-a-bitch had dropped two thousand pounds of records on my face. It suddenly dawned on me why he'd been so wary whenever I was around him. He had good reason to be wary of me, as I planned to show him.

I tore up Westwood Boulevard, burning rubber as I

turned right into English Woods. I jogged left again down the little side street leading to Philo's apartment house. The pimp-mobile was still parked in front of the yellow-brick apartment building, along with another car, a Mazda Miata with a vanity plate.

"CUM 'N' GIT," Sherwood said, sounding the letters on the plate out like a dullard. "What could that mean, you think?"

"I think Philo's got company."

"Hate to interrupt him at his pleasures." Sherwood cracked open his door. "But I gotta think of my little pal and his poor, innocent sweetheart."

I got out on my side and together we walked up the path to the front door.

"Best let me knock," Sherwood said when we got inside the hall.

"Be my guest."

For once Sherwood's size was an advantage. I stood behind him while he knocked on Philo's door.

A few moments later Philo opened it. "You again!" he said bitterly. "Ain't you bothered me enough tonight?"

"Perhaps I have," Sherwood said diplomatically. "But there is another party here who would like a word."

Waving his hand graciously he stepped away, revealing me.

One look at my face and Philo tried to slam the door shut. I got a leg through and pushed, but Philo was strong as a bear. Inside the apartment I heard a woman say, "Philo, honey, *what* is going on?"

"Shut up, Yolanda!" he shouted. "And give me a hand here."

I felt another hundred pounds or so of weight hit the door. I glanced over at Sherwood, who was watching the tussle with amusement.

"You want to give me some help, Sherwood?"

"Ah, I guess so, although I have never been one to believe in solving problems by a resort to brute force."

"Just push!" I shouted.

Putting his huge hands up to the door, Sherwood pushed.

The damn thing practically flew off its hinges, sending Philo and his half-naked girlfriend to the living room floor. I pulled the Airweight from my pocket and yanked Philo to his feet, shoving the two-inch barrel up his left nostril. The girlfriend shrieked and ran down the hall to the bedroom.

"Don't you call the cops, now, Yolanda!" Philo shouted after her.

He stared at the barrel in his nose and tried to smile. "Just be cool, brother."

"I didn't know you two were related, Harry," Sherwood said, plopping down on the sofa. "That was a mighty attractive girl you had in here, Philo. Mighty attractive."

"You motherfucker," he said, glancing furiously over at Sherwood. "You said you'd keep this tight."

Sherwood shrugged. "I lied."

Philo looked back at me. "Now, just take that piece out of my nose and let's sit down and talk."

"You dropped a bookcase on me," I said to him.

"How'd I know it was you? I didn't know it was you."

"You knew." I gave the barrel a twist.

"You guys want to hear something?" Sherwood asked. "I got a copy of *Gaîté Parisienne* back home that's damn fine listening."

"Son-of-a . . ." Philo muttered.

"Why'd Sheila give you a key, Philo?" I said. "Why'd she have you rob her own house?"

Philo just glared at me.

"Don't fuck with me," I said, jamming the barrel farther up his nose.

Philo winced. "She needed the money for something," he said sullenly.

"For what?" I gave him another little twist.

"A guy!" he shouted. "Some dude she knew was squeezing her for bread."

"It was Adams, wasn't it?"

"I told you before I don't know no Adams," Philo said. "This guy's name was Detroit. Bobby Detroit."

I pulled the gun out of his nose, and Philo slapped a hand to his nostril.

"You got my nose bleeding, you motherfucker," he said, blotting his nostril with the lapel of his velvet robe.

"I'm going to have you bleeding all over the goddamn house if you don't give me straight answers."

Philo gave me an ugly look, then sank down slowly on the arm of the couch.

"You know, Philo," I said, "I'm already having trouble with your story. Even if Sheila did need money, why would she pick a jive-ass nitwit like you to help her?"

"Nitwit!" Philo's eyes went almost completely white. "I'll get my nine out and fatten your white ass up, motherfucker!"

"Perhaps another taste of the gun, Harry?" Sherwood volunteered.

In spite of the fact that I was holding a pistol on him Philo lunged at Loeffler—twisting around and diving across the couch with his arms out and his fingers spread like talons. I grabbed him by the collar and pulled him back, while Sherwood looked on placidly.

"You cocksucker!" Philo shouted, trying to jerk loose from the hold I had on him. "Lying, conniving, racist mother."

"That's rather a bold statement," Sherwood said, "coming from a thief."

Philo laughed bitterly. "After all the vinyl you done stole from me, and you're calling me a thief!"

"There's a difference between trading and stealing."

"Yeah," Philo said. "When you're white, it's called trading."

Clearly I'd lost control of the situation—and I was the guy with the gun.

"Cool it!" I said. "Both of you."

Sherwood ducked his head and, after a moment, Philo sat down on the arm of the sofa.

"Now, let's get back to the point here, O.K.?" I said, pocketing the pistol. "Why did Sheila pick you to rob her house?"

Philo let out a long sigh. "I owed her something, O.K.?"

"Like what?"

He glanced up the hallway at the door behind which his ladylove was hidden. Lowering his voice to a hair above a whisper, he said, "Me and Sheila used to have a thing."

"A thing?"

"A love thing."

Christ, I said to myself. Another one.

"Correct me if I'm wrong, Harry," Sherwood said. "But Sheila *is* Jewish, isn't she?"

"Shut up, Sherwood," I said to him.

To Philo, I said, "When did you and Sheila . . . when were you together?"

Philo sighed again. " 'Bout two and half, three years ago. She sandwiched me in 'tween Pavel and Larry."

I laughed. "She told you about them?"

"When it comes to fucking, Sheila don't leave very much at home."

"So she gave you a key to the basement and told you to steal Leon's records?"

"She even told me which ones to take. She had this dude lined up in White Oak bought 'em off me, no questions asked. I got about two grand for her."

"Two grand!" Sherwood boomed. "You were robbed."

Philo just shook his head.

"How much of that money did you keep?" I asked.

"Not a dime, jack. I gave it all to her friend."

"Detroit?"

"When that long, tall, lying ass," he said, nodding at Sherwood, "told me she'd been snatched, I figured it had to be Detroit. She was sure as hell scared of him."

"You met Detroit?"

"Naw. Just dropped the green off at his motel. She thought Detroit would leave her alone if she give him that bread. It hurt her to steal Leon's discs though. She knew how tasty they was to him. But the way things stood she didn't have a choice. She give me a copy of that house key 'bout a week ago and phoned me up when she and Leon was out of their crib. Even told me to leave a couple of record jackets on the floor—make it look like Sherwood done it."

"A woman's wiles," Sherwood said with disappointment. "I thought she liked me."

"Give me a break," I said to him. "Where's Detroit's motel?"

"In Reading," Philo said. "A shit hole called the Sleepy Bear."

# 18

**IT MIGHT HAVE BEEN A DUMP,** but the Sleepy Bear was still a couple of steps up from Bob Adams's digs at the Lincoln. It was a fifties-style, single-story, L-shaped motel with a vaguely Batesian feel to it. A pillared awning ran around the front with the rooms set back about six feet under the awning—each one with the same black metal door and heavily draped picture window. Each one a winner, according to the neon sign out front.

Around one-thirty that Monday morning we pulled into the lot. Me, Philo, and Sherwood. I needed Philo for the Sleepy Bear, but I'd tried to drop Sherwood back at his house before heading out to the motel. He told me he wouldn't dream of it.

"I teach Aristotle to teenagers, Harry," he said. "I need the break."

It was thoroughly unprofessional to take either one

of them with me. But Sherwood was big enough to help me kick down a door, and if that didn't work Philo knew how to slip through a locked one.

It had started to snow again on the way out the interstate, and it was coming down pretty hard as the three of us sat there, staring through the windshield at the glassed-in booth that was the Sleepy Bear's sleepy-looking front office.

"Should we call the police?" Sherwood asked.

"Better make sure he's here first." I turned to Philo, who was crammed in the Pinto's backseat. "You don't know which room he's in, do you?"

Philo shook his head, no. "I just dropped the bread at the desk."

"Why don't you do that one more time?" I said.

"Ain't got no dough."

I dug a greasy envelope out of the glove compartment and shoved the Pinto's owner's manual into it. "Now, you got dough," I said, slapping the envelope into Philo's hand. "Only this time I want you to watch the clerk—see which box she puts the envelope in."

"Why don't we just go up there and ask which room the guy's in?" Sherwood said.

"Because they won't always give you the room number," I said. "They'll ring 'em up first. And we don't want that."

Philo shook his head. "Man, I'm doing a lot of work for a coupla strange white men."

Squeezing out of the backseat he trotted across the lot into the Sleepy Bear's office. Through the windshield we watched him go up to the front desk. A sluggish-looking woman in a tartan-plaid dress took the envelope and stowed it behind her in one of the letterboxes. Philo tipped his tam and came back out to the car.

"Seventeen," he said, breathing smoke from the cold. "Guess that must be 'round to the right there."

I started the Pinto up and coasted around the short wall of an aboveground pool. There were no lights on in any of the rooms on that side of the motel and no Cadillac with Kentucky plates outside Number 17, but that didn't mean that Bobby Detroit wasn't home. If he had a brain in his head, he would have dumped the car hours ago. He could be sitting in the room with his hands behind his head, high on an ampoule of morphine.

Where Sheila was sitting—or lying—in the picture I'd conjured up was a different question. Maybe in a closet. Maybe tied to the bed. Either way could present a problem. If I busted in on Bob, there would be violence —without question, violence. And Sheila could end up getting hurt.

Sherwood must have been thinking the same thing I was, because he said, "We should call the police," again with a little more urgency in his voice.

Only I wasn't so sure the police were a good idea— and not just because of the promise I'd made to Leon. Bob Adams a.k.a. Ross Finley a.k.a. Bobby Detroit was at the end of his rope—a two-time loser with charges of kidnapping and aggravated murder hanging over his head. I didn't see him surrendering himself or giving Sheila up to a police negotiator. He had a score to settle with her, anyway. My guess was that if the cops showed up he'd kill her—if he hadn't killed her already.

"Let's make sure he's in there, first," I finally said.

Sherwood asked, "How?"

"Anybody got a pick?"

I heard Philo sigh. "Here." He handed me a chain full of lever-type tension wrenches.

"My Lord," Sherwood said, "where'd you git something like that, Phi?"

"I use 'em to adjust my ax."

"I could use 'em to adjust a few things myself," Sherwood said thoughtfully. "Perhaps we should start thinking in terms of a trade."

"You got the last thing you're ever gonna get outta me," Philo told him.

Opening the glove compartment I dug through the debris and found a half-full pint of Scotch wedged way in the back. I took it out, gargled and swallowed a shot, and poured the rest of the liquor on my coat.

"Oh, man," I heard Philo say, "what a waste of good whiskey."

I messed up my hair, tore my collar open, and turned to the two of them.

"How do I look?"

"Drunk?" Sherwood said.

"Good. You two wait here."

"Watch your back," Philo said.

I patted my coat—the Airweight was still in my pocket—opened the car door and staggered out of the Pinto over to Number 17. I made a lot of noise outside the motel room door—enough to alert Bob that a guest was coming—then got out Philo's picks and started working the lock.

There wasn't a sound from inside the room. And there should have been, considering the racket I'd raised.

After a moment the lock sprung and the door swung open. The light beneath the awning fell across another empty, unmade hotel-style bed. I glanced back at the Pinto—where Sherwood and Philo were pressed to the windshield like kids at a peep show—then took the pistol from my coat pocket and crept into the motel room.

I could tell from the sound of the place that there was no one home. And a quick look confirmed it. Surprisingly I did find a few items in plain sight. A spike, swabbed with cotton, was sitting on the dresser by the bed next to an empty ampoule of morphine. Ol' Bob had apparently loaded up on some of his pharmaceuticals before going out. I also found a brassiere and a pair of torn panties on the floor outside the john. There were bloodstains on the bra. Enough to give the creeps.

It looked as if Bobby Detroit *had* been keeping Sheila in the motel room and that he'd taken her with him when he'd gone.

I went back to the motel room door and beckoned to my two volunteers. I saw them turn and look at each other uncertainly, then both of them got out of the car and came over to the door.

"He ain't home, huh?" Sherwood said, breathing smoke and slapping his arms against the cold.

I shook my head. "Come on inside."

They stepped through the door and I shut it behind them, closing out the cold wind and the noise of the Reading Road traffic.

I flipped a switch by the door and the room lit up. It had looked better in the dark. The unmade bed sat on the left wall, flanked by nightstands with lava lamps on them. A Heart-Mart bureau sat on the opposite wall. There were doors to a closet and to the john. And that was it.

"Ain't even got color TV," Philo said.

"What now?" Sherwood said, sinking down on the bed.

"We search the place."

Philo snickered. "There ain't any place to search."

"That's what Gertrude Stein said about Oakland," Sherwood said.

"There's the bureau, the closet, and the bed," I told them.

"And I suppose you're gonna get the nigger to crawl under the bed, right?" Philo said.

"I'll take the bed. Philo, you take the closet. And Sherwood, the bureau."

"I ain't so sure this a three-man job," Sherwood said, standing up with a grunt.

He seemed a little disappointed, as if he'd been looking forward to gunplay and bloody death. Philo just looked bored.

We searched the room—me and my forensic team. Sherwood found a few items of men's clothing in the bureau drawers—underwear, a couple of dress shirts, trousers, and a tie. He also found Sheila's wallet mixed in among Adams's socks. Everything but the driver's license had been removed from it—credit cards, Social Security, the works.

Philo found a piece of knotted rope and some gauze and tape in the closet. There were blond hairs adhering to the tape and what looked like a small bloodstain on one of the walls. That's where Adams had apparently been keeping Sheila—on the floor of the closet. And it didn't appear as if he'd been keeping her well.

The bloodstain upset Philo, who really did have a sense of loyalty to Sheila Mozkowski.

"That motherfucker," he said, his eyes flashing. "I'm gonna cut his junkie heart out when I catch up with him."

Sherwood nodded. "Yes, but how are we going to do that?"

That was the question, all right. And then I found the answer.

I hadn't come up with a matchbook in the Lincoln Hotel. But I sure as hell found one in the Sleepy Bear, between the bed and the right-hand nightstand.

"A clue!" Sherwood said, rubbing his hands.

Philo glared at him. "You're a cold son-of-a-bitch, Sherwood. That lady's probably riding around in that fucker's trunk right now, and you're making jokes."

Sherwood actually blushed. "I'm sorry, Philo. My sense of humor was misplaced."

"At birth," Philo said acidly.

I took the matchbook over to the lamp. It was just a plain white book, without any ads or slogans on it. But inside the cover someone had written a phone number and a name, *555-6295, Lorette.*

"It's just like a detective story," Sherwood said.

It was a little too much like a detective story for my taste.

"Think we should call?" Philo asked.

"Let's find out who the phone number belongs to first."

# 19

**WE DROVE TO MY OFFICE** in the Riorley. All three of us, at two-thirty in the morning. Me smelling like a liquor store break-in, Philo looking like he was being dragged in chains, and Sherwood chipper as ever.

"This is rather exciting," Sherwood said as we came through the door into my chilly office. "A detective's office in the middle of a January night. A hot case to solve."

He rubbed his hands together vigorously.

Philo gave him an acid look. "You're an asshole, you know that?"

"There you go name-calling again. I'm not the one who called you a nitwit."

"No, you the one I'm gonna kill soon as I find my razor. Cocksucker, you went and told this other fool about those damn records. Now I gotta stomp around in the snow all hours of the night. I didn't even get to tell Yolanda where I was going. And I got a gig tomorrow at the Blue Wisp!"

"You can go home if you want, Philo," I said. "We can handle it from here."

Philo's face dropped. "You ain't gonna need me no more?"

"You said you wanted to leave."

Philo made a growling noise, like he was trying to clear his foot out of his mouth. "Guess I'll stick around till we find Sheila. Gone this far. Few hours more don't make no difference."

Sherwood smiled and clapped him on the shoulder. "That's the spirit, brother."

"Get your hands off me!" Philo said. "And I ain't your brother."

"It was a figure of speech. Obviously I do not consider you my brother."

"Can it," I said before they could start up again.

It was a weird case.

I went over to my file drawer and pulled out the reverse telephone directory. Slapping the thing down on my desk I thumbed through it, looking for 555-6295.

"That's a Northern Kentucky exchange," Philo said.

I flipped back to the Northern Kentucky section. And there it was. If I'd had half a brain I would have thought of it hours before.

"Well, I'll be damned," Sherwood said, grinning. "That must be his mother."

Or his sister or his cousin or his grandma or his ex-wife. But it sure as hell was an Adams. Lorette Adams,

56 Boone Street in Bromley—where Bob had robbed the pharmacy.

Philo gave me a disgusted look. "Why didn't you think of that before?"

"Because *I'm* a nitwit."

"Yes, you are," Philo said.

"I'd have to concur," Sherwood said.

Before leaving the office I opened the safe and took the three aluminum bricks of money out. I had a feeling I might need them before the night was done.

"What's that?" Philo asked, as I shoved them into my overcoat pockets.

"The stuff that dreams are made of," I told him.

To get to Bromley, Kentucky, we had to cross the I-75 bridge over the Ohio and turn off at the Ludlow exit, then follow Route 8 as it circled through Highland Heights, down through Ludlow to Bromley itself. Ludlow and Bromley were river towns and 8 hewed to the river as it passed through them, ducking away to accommodate a hill or two but always coming back to the Ohio's bank before long.

It was dark and cold but you could feel the river out in the darkness beyond the fringe of houses and, every once in a while, you could see it through an open lot or a break in the buildings—fog-shrouded and icy and smeared with a few early morning water lights. The fog began to creep onto the roadway at Ludlow, which was lower ground and closer to the Ohio. Mixing with the snow that had begun to fall again, it lent the last half of the ride a spooky feel of danger.

"I've always loved the fog," Sherwood said.

Philo snickered. "That's 'cause it's white, like them sheets your daddy used to wear."

"My father was a town marshal in Corbin, Kentucky," Sherwood said with great dignity. "A peace officer who despised the KKK, as I myself do."

"I'm surprised to hear you say that, Sherwood," I said, twitting him.

"You are, are you? Do you think a man like Wagner would have had any truck with those mindless hooligans? He despised the mob. It is the individual alone who can scale the creative heights. Art, Harry, music—that's what I believe in."

"Me, too," Philo said. "It don't hurt to have a good system in your crib, though."

"No, it doesn't," Sherwood said, descending from the heights.

The fog got so dense at Bromley I had to slow down to make out the road signs. There wasn't much more than road signs to Bromley, anyway. A gas station, a small retail strip of storefronts with names like Polly's Manicure and Styling and French's Variety Five and Dime and Jack's Cat Fish Farm. It was a little like a time warp—a main street right out of the thirties, shrouded in fog. Even the police station looked dated. It was on the bottom floor of a KOC hall.

"Do either of you guys see a Boone Street?" I asked.

They both craned their necks.

"There's one coming up here on the left called Main," Philo said.

"Let's try it."

I turned onto Main, driving back into the residential section of Bromley. The first crossing street was Duluth, the second Anaconda. The third was the charm.

"Boone!" Sherwood said, rubbing his hands together.

I turned right onto Boone and slowed down to a crawl. Main Street ran uphill, so there was less fog in the air and if you squinted hard you could make out the house numbers in the headlights.

"Forty-four," Philo said.

"We're getting close," Sherwood said. "It'll be on the right."

Fifty-six was a white clapboard, one-story shack, running lengthwise from the street. There was a grass lot beside it with a rusted pickup sitting in it, jacked-up on cement blocks. I didn't see a car in the driveway or the roofed port.

"Now what?" Sherwood said eagerly.

He wasn't talking about calling the police anymore. Even Philo looked a little excited.

"Let's go in."

"Yeah," Sherwood said.

"Yeah," Philo echoed.

I parked the car on Boone, and together the three of us walked up the driveway through the thin shreds of fog to Lorette Adams's front door, which was located midway down the right side of the house. There was a little Dutch roof over the stoop and a couple of picture windows on either side, drawn with curtains.

I took out Philo's pick and worked on the lock.

"What if it's deadbolt?" Philo whispered.

"Then we'll try a window," I whispered back.

But it wasn't a deadbolt. The lock clicked and the door fell open at my touch.

There wasn't a light on inside, but my eyes were used to the dark by then. I put a hand to my lips, signaling silence, took the .38 out of my pocket, and stepped through the door into a small hallway that ran the length of the house.

"Stay here," I whispered to Sherwood and Philo.

I went down the hall to the left. It was so narrow I felt like I was walking through a Pullman car. The hall emptied into a medium-sized living room, furnished in what looked in the near-dark like near-antiques. A bit of street light seeping through the white curtains lit up a mantelpiece with family photographs on it—like Le-Roy's mantel.

I turned around and walked back up the hall to the other end of the house. At the back was a kitchen—painted wood cabinets and fifties-style appliances—with another short hall opening off it to a bath and a bedroom. Both doors were open.

I cocked the pistol and stepped into the bedroom. It was clearly a woman's room, fitted out with lace valences on the windows and a lace doily on the mahogany headboard of an old open-spring bed. A dressing table sat opposite the bed with a glass dish in its center, full of makeup. There was no one in the room.

I glanced into the john. It was empty too.

The whole house appeared to be empty.

It wasn't until I turned on the lights that I figured out why.

There was a mail chute off the kitchen door and a huge pile of unopened letters and advertisements sitting beneath it—some of them postmarked better than a week before.

"She's out of town," Sherwood said, coming into the kitchen. Philo was right behind him.

"Spread out," I said, "and search this damn place."

We searched the first floor for almost half an hour —living room, kitchen, bedroom, john—sifting through Lorette Adams's furnishings and belongings for anything that would lead us to Bob or to Sheila. It wasn't until we got down to the basement that we found what we were looking for—and afraid of.

It was a large unfinished room with stone walls, cement floor, and steel girders jacked up with two-by-sixes to bolster the upper story. We could hear the hum of the furnace from the landing. The very fact that the damn thing was running meant that someone had been in the house since Lorette Adams had left town. As soon as Philo flipped on the light switch, we figured out who that someone was. There was a rope tied to one of the girders at the foot of the staircase, and beneath it, on the floor, Sheila's torn, bloodstained muumuu.

"Oh, man," Philo said, turning away. "Oh, man."

Sherwood looked away, too.

There was a good deal of blood on the floor, and on the rope itself—too much for anyone to have survived the wound it came from.

"This is murder," Sherwood said in a hollow voice.

"He ain't gonna get away with it," Philo said angrily.

"We'll see to that," I promised him.

# 20

**AFTER WE GOT OVER** the initial shock of seeing all the blood, we went through the basement carefully—or as carefully as two amateur and one semiprofessional detectives could. I told Philo and Sherwood not to touch anything with their hands, and they were good about it —especially Philo, who had had some experience pilfering other people's property. A few minutes into the search, Philo found another spike and an ampoule of morphine on the floor by the furnace. And a few minutes after that, Sherwood found the mother lode—a duffel bag filled with ampoules of morphine—hidden badly under some loose boards and broken pieces of drywall in a heap near the back wall. With the exception of the whereabouts of the principal actors, we seemed to have wrapped up the entire case—in the space of three hours.

"What do you think he done with the body?" Sherwood asked.

I shook my head. "She could be buried out in the yard. Or he could have dropped her in the river. Hell, there's hill country not too many miles from here. He could have stashed her up there."

Before abandoning the search, I slipped on my winter gloves and went through the contents of the duffel bag—to see if I could find any further clues to Bob's whereabouts. It seemed a mite piggish, seeing how generous Adams had already been with clues. But I made the search anyway and, sure enough, found Bob Adams's picture ID and a few thousand dollars—nowhere close to the hundred and forty grand that was missing—mixed in with the stolen drugs. I also found a bloody hatchet with blond hairs adhering to the blade.

"I guess this is what happened to the body," I said, holding the gruesome thing up to the light.

Sherwood wouldn't look at the hatchet. And when Philo saw it he got so angry he kicked a dent the size of a basketball in the hot water heater. It was a murder scene, and we were traipsing through it like schoolgirls.

"We're gonna have to call the cops, Harry." All the fun was gone from Sherwood's voice. "This ain't no game."

He was right.

We left everything as we'd found it and trudged wearily back upstairs to the living room. Outside the winter storm was rattling the windows with both hands. I glanced at my watch, which was showing 4:30 A.M., and thought about Leon Tubin, sitting half-awake by the phone, waiting for a call that would only prove to be a cruel hoax.

Philo sat down in a bentwood rocker and put his head in his hands. He'd been badly shaken by what we'd uncovered, but then he had the best reason to be upset —Sheila Mozkowski had been his lover. Sherwood was also uncharacteristically subdued. Walking over to the fireplace he picked up one of the photographs lining the mantel and stared at it dully. After a second or two, his pensive expression changed to shock.

"Good Lord," he said with a gasp, "this here kid looks like Richard Wagner."

"It's Adams," I said, staring at the photo over his shoulder—a picture of a teenaged Adams standing beside a gaunt, white-haired woman, whom I took to be his mother, Lorette.

"It cain't be," Sherwood said with pain in his voice.

"Well it is."

Shaking his head Sherwood put the picture back on the mantel, walked over to a floral-print couch with doilies on the cushions, and sank down in the middle of it.

"That is the unkindest cut of all," he said miserably.

Raising his head Philo looked over at him angrily. "He cares more about that Wagner than he does about poor Sheila."

"It's his religion," I said to Philo.

"That don't make it right. You gonna call Leon?"

"Yeah. I guess I have to," I said with a sigh.

"It's pitiful," Philo said. "Just pitiful. She was a damn fine woman."

From his trough of despond Sherwood looked up

with a spark of hope in his eyes. "Maybe Adams didn't do it. Maybe it was somebody else."

"Who didn't look like Wagner?" I said, glaring at him. "You're reaching, Sherwood."

He nodded heavily. "I guess I am. Only you know what I don't understand? How come he wrote that phone number and the woman's name down in the matchbook? I mean he must've known his own mother's name. And why would he call her up, anyway, if she was out of town?"

It was actually a pretty good question. "Maybe he wasn't sure she was out of town. Maybe he wanted to check on her before . . . using the basement."

"That don't explain him writing down a name he oughta know by heart," Sherwood said, warming to the subject. "And another thing. How come we keep finding all this stuff so easy? It don't happen that way on TV. I mean why would Adams leave all them drugs on the floor with the ax and the money and his own ID mixed up with 'em? I don't know much about crooks, but I'd say it was damn foolish of him, unless he was planning to come back and git all of it."

It was another good point—one that had already occurred to me.

"Maybe we should stick around," Philo said.

"Maybe we should," I agreed.

———

I found a phone in an old-fashioned mahogany phone niche by the fireplace. While Philo and Sherwood were bickering in the kitchen, I called Leon's house.

" 'Bout damn time," LeRoy said when he picked up.

"Something's happened?"

"Hell, yes, something's happened," he said excitedly. "That son-of-a-bitch Adams called about an hour ago. He wants his money—and he wants it quick. He said for Leon to meet him in the Turfway racetrack parking lot at six this morning. Make the exchange for Sheila."

"I'll meet him there."

"Harry, he's expectin' a hundred and seventy grand and Leon."

"Well, he's gonna get thirty and me," I said.

"You find something out?" LeRoy said, picking up on my grim tone of voice.

I started to tell him about the motel room and Lorette Adams's basement, then thought better of it. Maybe it was the hour or just a momentary weakness, but I'd been infected by some of Sherwood's skepticism. Given his long arrest sheet I knew that Bob Adams was no mastermind, and it was clear from the empty ampoules we kept finding that he'd been stoned on morphine most of the previous day and night. But even a dumb, stoned junkie-thug should have been more careful than Adams had been. The bastard had left a trail that children could have followed—and had.

On the other hand, I reminded myself, Adams had shown unmistakable signs of stupidity in the past—notably when he'd let Sheila set him up at the Quality Court in '88 and when he'd robbed the pharmacy in Bromley on Saturday night and then used the same car to abduct the girl. Also he didn't know that Leon had a detective working for him—and two ace sidekicks. He hadn't planned on us following him. Perhaps he hadn't planned anything at all—outside of snatching poor Sheila. Which itself might have been a spur of the moment thing, following so hard on the drugstore robbery. Once he'd taken her, Adams might have figured on slopping his way through until he got the ransom money.

Still, sloppiness didn't explain the matchbook with Lorette Adams's name and number in it, or the bag of drugs and money and murder weapons and ID's he'd left at the murder scene. That went beyond sloppy—it was criminal. The whole night had been too much like a detective story, in which clues follow each other in bang-bang order.

If I'd thought *that* through I could have solved the case right there, on the spot. But I was too tired and upset by the brutality of Sheila's murder and worried about my early morning rendezvous with Mr. Adams to make the right connections.

Both Sherwood and Philo wanted to go with me to the racetrack rendezvous. For different reasons.

"I wanta kill the motherfucker with my bare hands," Philo said furiously.

"I want to ask him if he knows what irreparable harm he has done to the memory of a great man," Sherwood said. "Then I would be in favor of killing him, too."

We were unanimous on killing him. But I figured it was best to let the law do it—once we had him cornered.

"I'm gonna give him the money," I told them. "Since he's expecting one hundred and seventy grand, he's probably not going to like it when I only give him thirty. If he starts trouble, I'll try to nail him at the track. If he's willing to settle for the smaller amount, I'll let him come back here to pick up his duffel bag. You guys call the cops and have them waiting here at the house. O.K.?"

"Do we synchronize watches?" Sherwood said.

"It's . . ." I glanced at my watch. "Five-thirty. At six sharp you call the cops and tell them to come here to the house. Right?"

They both nodded.

"You know, Harry," Sherwood said, "however stupid, this fellow is quite dangerous and more than a little nuts."

"I can take care of myself, Sherwood."

"Just . . . thought I'd mention it," he said, ducking his head.

"Now, don't forget," I said. "Make the call at six sharp."

"Take care, brother," Philo said, pointing a finger at me.

"I plan to."

# 21

IT WAS SIX on the very cold nose of a foggy Monday morning when I pulled into the parking lot of the Turfway racetrack in Latonia, Kentucky—a little town about ten miles due south of Bromley whose sole industry was the racing of horses and the fleecing of the men and women who bet on them. The fog in the Turfway lot was so thick that the only things I could see clearly were the light poles rising above the mist like umbrellas on a beach. I turned on my car lights to bright and coasted through the dark, searching for a murderer in a stolen Cadillac.

Only an idiot like Bobby Detroit would have picked a fogbound parking lot for a ransom exchange. After ten minutes of aimless cruising I had the feeling I was going to have to get out of the car and start shouting his name, like a deckhand sounding depth from the bow of a riverboat. But it didn't come to that.

After circling the lot two more times—or circling something, it might have been a single lamppost for all I knew—I spotted a pair of headlights flashing in the dark and mist. It was six-fifteen by then.

I coasted toward the flashing lights and stopped about twenty feet away from them. Between the high beams of our cars and the arc lights overhead I could see the Cadillac fairly clearly, and Bobby Adams sitting inside it—the man with Richard Wagner's face.

I got out of the Pinto and stood behind the driver's side door. After a moment Adams got out of the Caddie. The guy was so stoned and overweight, he had to struggle to make it out the door. His head was enormous, so larded with fat that his chins and the dewlaps of his jaws hung down around his neck like loose lining. He looked like a man wearing a sack with a face painted on it. Wan and bilious and crazy.

I watched his hands closely, expecting to see a pistol or a shotgun. But he wasn't holding a weapon. In fact he looked too stoned and out of shape to do anything but stare straight ahead and wobble. It came to me that even if I didn't get Adams or the cops somehow missed him at Boone Street, he was going to kill himself with morphine before the week was out.

"Who the fuck are you?" he said in a slurred, heavily inebriated voice.

"I'm here for Leon. I'm a friend of his."

"I told *him* to come, goddamnit!" Adams shouted.

In the fog he sounded miles away, although we were only a few feet apart.

"You worked him over so badly he couldn't make the trip," I told him.

Bob Adams laughed with crude satisfaction. "The little dipshit got in my way."

At that moment *I* would have liked to have gotten in Bob Adams's way. But I had to think beyond what he'd done to Leon—and what we'd found in Lorette Adams's basement.

"You got my dough?" Adams called out.

He said it like it had been *his* from the start. If it had been, he'd taken his revenge many times over on Sheila Mozkowski with that ax.

"Right here."

I held up one of the aluminum foil bricks.

"Bring it over."

"Show me Sheila first."

"What're you talking about?" Adams said sharply. "You get Sheila back *after* I get the money."

"Back from the dead, huh?"

"The bitch ain't dead," he said cockily—figuring I couldn't know better. "Just give me the fuckin' money. Or you'll never see her again."

"There wasn't a hundred and seventy thousand left."

Adams's wan, paunchy, sacklike face bunched up, as if someone had pulled a drawstring at his neck. Puckering his chewed-over mouth he glared at me savagely. "You get smart, mister, and I'll kill you. I've killed men before."

"I've only got thirty grand."

"Thirty grand!" Bobby Adams's hand shot to his

coat pocket. He pulled out a .357 magnum and pointed it at me unsteadily.

"This is the last time I let Sheila double-cross me!" he screamed.

And I knew that he meant business. I ducked down behind the open car door, fumbling with the .38 in my pocket. And then a very peculiar thing happened.

Lights went on—all over the dark, misty parking lot, burning through the fog and the night with the intensity of kliegs.

"What the fuck?" I heard Bobby Adams shout.

I peered around the car door and saw blue bubbletops flashing from just about every direction. I figured that Sherwood and Philo had decided to send the cops to Turfway when Bobby Adams hadn't shown up back at Boone Street. And I was glad they had.

Wide-eyed, Adams spun around in a full circle, staring in stoned disbelief as the cop cars came pouring in on him.

"Shit! Shit! Shit!" he shouted, and hopped into the Caddie.

He started the car up without closing the door and took off with a squeal of rubber, slamming directly into one of the nearby light poles. The Caddie's radiator went up with a hiss of steam. I heard the light pole crack and watched it fall into the misty lot, exploding in a shower of sparks when the bulb head hit the concrete.

Adams was out of the car by then. His face bleeding, the magnum in his hand. He waved the gun wildly and started shooting at the oncoming police cars. A couple of the closest ones jerked to a stop—the cops spilling out the doors like Marines hitting a beach. They began to return fire immediately with their 9-mm Smiths—thirty-round clips that went off like machine guns and had muzzle blasts like tracers. It was dark and foggy so no one was taking very sure aim.

Adams kept spinning around and shooting until he was finally hit. His face went white and he plunged a hand inside his overcoat, tearing it open with a groan. Then another round hit him full in the shoulder. He went down to his knees like he'd been standing under a safe, dropped the gun in front of him, and fell forward on his hands.

I waited until I was sure that he was down for good, then stood up and walked over to where he was crouching on the pavement. The cops came up too. One of them kicked Bobby Adams's gun away.

"Thanks," I said to the cop.

The cop nodded brusquely, holstering his weapon.

I looked down at Adams.

"What did you do with her body, Bob?" I asked him.

He shook his head. There was blood dripping from his mouth and it splashed onto the pavement on either side of him.

Looking up at me, he laughed through bloody teeth. "You'll never find her," he said.

He dropped his head again and began to pant like a sick animal.

An ambulance came screaming up and paramedics surrounded Bobby Adams. I went back to the Pinto. I was still holding one of the aluminum bricks in my left hand. I stared at it stupidly, then put it in my coat pocket.

The cop whom I'd thanked came up beside me. "It's a good thing we got that call."

I nodded. "Good thing for me."

"We're gonna want to ask you a few questions, mister," he said in a no-nonsense voice.

"I figured," I said, turning toward him.

He was a Bromley cop with an ex-Marine's granite, clean-shaven face.

"My friends had nothing to do with it," I said, thinking about Sherwood and Philo.

"Which friends are those?" he asked.

"The two at the Boone Street house, where we found the murder weapon. The ones who called you."

"Uh-huh." He pulled out his cuffs and snapped them around my wrists. "Just a formality."

"I know. I used to be a cop."

His granite look softened into limestone. "What department?"

"Cincinnati. I worked for the DA. Check with Al Foster at the CPD."

"I'll do that," he said.

Turning me around he led me over to a squad car. To my right I could see the paramedics putting Bob Adams into the ambulance.

"He kidnapped a woman and killed her," I said.

"Killed a druggist, too."

The cop stowed me in the backseat, pushing my head down so I wouldn't hit the top of the car door. I was very tired and cold and all I really wanted to do was go to sleep. But I knew that sleep was hours away. For me, Sherwood, and Philo the day had just began.

**204**

**22**

BOB ADAMS'S MOTHER, Lorette, came back home later that morning. She'd been in Florida on a getaway plan. Bobby had boosted her to a ticket the week before—using some of the money that Sheila had given him from the sale of the stolen records.

Lorette thought Bobby was such a good boy. Troubled, but fundamentally a good boy. And she couldn't understand why the cops had all those backhoes and dozers plowing up her yard.

I heard about Lorette from a cop in the Bromley PD's detention room, where I spent most of the day, along with Sherwood Loeffler and Philo Ives. I also heard that Bobby Adams was expected to live, but not expected to cooperate. The police had questioned him in the Emergency Room and later in the day after he came out of surgery. But he wouldn't say a word about Sheila's whereabouts—or about anything else.

"Man, he was pissed off," one of the cops laughed. "Like the world had gone against him."

Philo didn't weather the morning and afternoon particularly well. Cops made him nervous. And later in the day I found out why.

"Do you know Cincinnati's got twelve outstanding capiases on you?" a cop asked him.

"Me?" Philo said innocently.

"Don't give me that crap, boy."

He was a Kentucky cop and he liked making a black man squirm. So did Sherwood. But not that afternoon.

"Leave that man alone," he said, drawing himself up to his full six feet eight inches. "And quit calling him boy, or I will report you to the State Police Commission. This is not East L.A."

"Fuck you," the cop said.

"Is there a State Police Commission?" Sherwood asked after the cop left the room.

I laughed. "Yeah. But name-calling isn't one of their priorities."

"Oh, Lord," Philo said, holding his head in his hands. "I knew this would happen. It's what comes of messing with white men."

"I resent that," Sherwood snapped. "You should be grateful to me for defending you. I thought it was a mighty magnanimous gesture on my part."

Philo laughed weakly. "You big, tall ass."

Sherwood said, "When are they gonna let us out of here? I really should call my wife and my two adorable children."

"It may be a little while," I told him.

Around 3 P.M. that afternoon the cop with the stony face, who turned out to be a relatively decent guy named Luke Carson, came into the detention room with a reel-to-reel tape recorder in one hand and a box of tape in the other. The Bromley police had had our stories for several hours by then, so I knew that he wasn't going to tape any more statements.

"We're gonna release you men in about twenty minutes," he said. "All except for you."

He pointed at Philo, who groaned.

"The CPD wants to have a chat with you about some overdue parking tickets."

"We'll pay the fine, Officer," Sherwood said wearily.

"Two thousand six hundred and fifty dollars?" Carson said.

"Whoa!" Sherwood glanced at Philo. "What'd you do, Phi? Ram a school bus?"

"We'll take care of it," I said. "I'm sure Mr. Tubin will want to compensate Mr. Ives for his time."

"How 'bout my time?" Sherwood said, turning sulky.

"You got the record, Sherwood."

"Ah." He nodded as if that was just.

"I wouldn't tell Leon, though."

"I'll keep it under my hat," Sherwood said.

Poor Leon. I could only imagine how he'd reacted when the cops had come to his door to tell him about Sheila. The little man had lost everything—his stereo, his favorite records, and his one true love. Well, true at least in the spiritual sense. He was going to lose the thirty thousand dollars, too. The cops had confiscated the bricks as evidence for Bobby Adams's trial. They'd locked them in their own freezer for six to nine months, and it was more than likely that some efficient property clerk was already checking the serial numbers of those mint-fresh, consecutive bills to find out where they'd come from. Which probably meant they'd be lost forever.

Sergeant Carson set the tape recorder down on a steel table and took the spool of tape out of the box. "Before you men are released, I want you to listen to something. This is our 911 tape from Monday morning. Listen carefully and tell me if you recognize any of the voices."

He put the tape on the machine and started it up.

There was an electronic beep and a voice—Sherwood's voice—said: "Police Department? There has been a murder at 56 Boone Street. Please come at once. We have reason to believe that the murderer plans to return to the scene of the crime. Don't we, Phi?"

I heard Philo say, "Yeah!"

"So come at once," Sherwood said again. "This is not a joke! Even though it may seem like one. Believe me I have been the butt of many jokes, so I know the impulse to simply rise above . . ."

The cop hit the stop switch on the recorder then fast forward. "This goes on for some time."

"I was just trying to be thorough," Sherwood said testily.

The cop pressed the rewind switch, then hit play.

"That call was 6 A.M. This next one you're gonna hear came in at 6:03."

There was another beep, then a voice I didn't recognize, a man's voice sounding muffled and thin, said: "There is a robbery in progress at Turfway racetrack. If you get there quickly, you'll catch the robber in the act. He's the same guy that killed the druggist in Bromley."

Carson hit the off switch.

"Well?"

The three of us looked at each other blankly.

"I've got no idea," Sherwood said.

"Me, neither," Philo said.

"I thought you guys sent the cops to Latonia," I said to them.

Sherwood shook his head. "It wasn't us, Harry. You gave us strict orders to have them come to Boone Street."

"It's a good thing that other call came in," Carson said to me. " 'Cause we didn't send anybody to Boone Street until after *you* told me about your pals."

"Why not?" Sherwood said with umbrage.

"We thought it was a crank call."

Philo laughed. "Big deal college professor."

"This is an outrage," Sherwood said, coloring. "This whole affair is an outrage. I intend to write the State Police Commission a detailed letter."

"You do that," Carson said. "Do you recognize the voice, Stoner?"

"No. It sounds like some guy who was trying to disguise his voice."

"That's what we think. We run traces on 911's automatically. This one came from a phone booth in Florence Mall—about three miles from Latonia. Do you think it's possible that this guy Adams had an accomplice?"

"Sure it's possible," I said. "But I wouldn't have any idea who it could be. It sure didn't look like he had anyone else with him, except for Sheila."

Sherwood held up a finger. "You're forgetting that matchbook."

The son-of-a-gun was right.

I said, "We found a matchbook in a Reading hotel room that Adams had been renting. Someone had written down the Boone Street telephone number and Lorette Adams's name inside it. My tall friend there thought it was suspicious because Adams wouldn't have written his own mother's name down as a reminder to himself."

"But he might have written it down if he was leaving a message for somebody else," Sherwood said triumphantly. "The real murderer."

He was going to rescue Wagner from the cloud of Bobby Adams, one way or another.

"It's an interesting theory," Carson said. "You have the matchbook?"

I dug it out of my coat.

"We'll try to lift prints, although you three clowns probably fucked it up pretty good. We'll also have Cincy check with the clerk at the motel. See if he saw anyone else coming or going out of Adams's room."

"May we leave, now?" Sherwood said with great dignity.

"Yeah, you can go."

We even managed to get Philo sprung before leaving the Bromley police station. I posted a 10 percent cash bond for him, and they released him into my custody.

"He's your ward now," Sherwood said as we drove back across the Clay-Wade-Bailey Bridge to Cincy. "Your own personal black ward."

He said it like it was something he'd always dreamed of owning. Philo was too tired, and too relieved, to riposte.

I dropped Philo at English Woods, then took Sherwood back to East Walnut Hills.

"You're gonna have some explaining to do," I said, as we pulled up in front of his house.

"My wife is very understanding," he said. But he looked a little nervous. The first time I'd seen him look truly nervous since I'd met him.

"Well, Harry . . ."

I shook his hand. "Sherwood, it has been a trip—as we used to say."

"Well, I never used to say that," he said. "In fact I wouldn't dream of saying something so stupid and cliché. Something that smacks of drugs and free love and living burials."

I drove off before he could get up a head of steam.

# 23

**THAT WAS MONDAY.**

Early on Tuesday morning I drove out to Leon's house in Saylor Park. I just hadn't had the guts to face him the night before, although I'd talked to him briefly on the phone from my apartment before collapsing with exhaustion around six Monday night.

Through LeRoy he'd asked whether there was any chance that Sheila was still alive.

"There's a chance," I told him. "Not a good chance. He shouldn't get his hopes up."

LeRoy told Leon what I said. And I heard him start to cry.

"Oh, Lord," LeRoy said. "This is pitiful. The most pitiful thing I ever did see."

"Stay with him, LeRoy," I said.

"Why sure I will."

212

That Tuesday morning it was my turn to comfort him. I pulled up in front of the little stucco house as I'd last done on Sunday night, when there had still been some hope for Sheila and Leon. A day and a half later, that hope was gone. By then the cops had visited Leon's house to take hair samples from Sheila's brushes and to check her medical and dental records. The preliminary autopsy report said that the hair and the blood on the ax matched Sheila's.

I went inside the house and found several of the other stereophiles gathered in the living room. LeRoy, Pavel, Dave Barber, Lawrence Peacock, Hank Diamond. Sherwood was conspicuously absent. They were putting Leon's stereo back together—trying to, anyway. I found it kind of touching, in an o/c way.

"It's beat-up," Peacock said, "but I think we'll get it functioning."

"Sure we will," LeRoy said cheerfully. "We're gonna clean up them records, too. Get him some music back. Leon's still got music."

It was a consolation. Maybe even a bigger one than I'd realized, because when I went back to the bedroom to pay my respects Leon looked red-eyed but resigned. He was reading that damn mystery book by the woman from Nome—just staring at the pages in a sort of a trance. When he saw me come through the door, he dropped the book with a sigh and picked up a pad and pencil. "Thank you for trying," he wrote.

"I'm sorry, man."

Leon started writing again. When he was done, he showed the pad to me.

"I had her for a little while. That's more than I

expected out of my life—a guy like me. I didn't think a woman like Sheila would ever love me. But she did."

"Yeah, she did."

He covered his eyes with his hands. "Sh' di'," he said in a broken voice.

I gave him a moment to recover.

"You'll be all right?"

He nodded, lowering his hand and wiping his eyes. "I'll be all right," he wrote. "But it won't ever be the same without her."

"Is there anything I can do?"

"Did all you could," Leon wrote. "I just hope she didn't suffer much."

She'd been killed with an ax so she'd suffered—much. But I didn't tell Leon that.

"Good-bye, Harry," he wrote. "I know we were a lot of trouble. Don't think badly of us. I'll always think of you fondly. You are a real friend."

I walked out of the bedroom, heavy of heart, past the music lovers busily rebuilding Leon's system, out into the cold bright January morning.

I stared at his white stucco house again for a brief minute, then got in the car and drove away.

———

Three days went by, and my business didn't improve. Jo Riley wasn't due home for another week. So I ended up with a lot of dead time on my hands—a lot of time to think about Leon and Sheila. About what I might have done differently—or the same. I'd given Sergeant Luke Carson a couple of calls—to see if the Bromley police made any progress finding Sheila's corpse or Adams's accomplice. I called him again that Friday morning, but he told me what I already knew.

"Adams could've dumped the body anywhere. The coroner says she probably died in the basement, judging from the amount of blood. What happened next, only Adams knows. And he's not talking."

"Still not talking?"

"I mean not a word. It's like he's taken a vow of silence. He won't even speak to a lawyer. He just sits there all day in the hospital like a guy who's already sitting on death row. Of course the fact that he's going cold turkey isn't improving his disposition."

"And the accomplice?"

"Same story. The motel clerk at the Sleepy Bear says she only saw the one guy go in the room—Adams. She positively ID'd him from a mug shot. So we're still in the dark about the tipster."

"Did the clerk see Sheila in the room?"

"No. He must've slipped her in late Saturday. Then took her over to Bromley the next morning and . . . done what he done."

"The fat, sick fuck."

"Yeah," Carson said. "All over money that wasn't even real."

"You're kidding," I said with surprise. "The thirty grand was counterfeit?"

"Every dime of it. Good counterfeit, too. That girl Sheila must've known some real crooks way back when."

"That's what caused all the trouble," I said grimly.

A couple of hours after I got off the phone with Carson I talked to another cop, Steve Torberg of the CPD Criminalistics squad. He was the guy with whom

I'd left the fingerprints—the prints I'd taken from Leon's basement on the Friday when I'd first gone out to the Saylor Park house. By then, I'd forgotten that I'd dropped the prints off. Torberg hadn't forgotten, though.

"Where the hell you been?" he asked. "I had results for you on Monday."

"I've been out of the office a lot," I told him.

"I'll say. You want to hear what I got?"

Not really, I said to myself. To him I said, "Shoot."

"It's probably not what you expected," Torberg said.

"And how is that?"

"Well, the prints from the cabinet and the door matched one of the comparison prints you brought in— the one you took from the woman, Sheila Mozkowski."

"So? That's exactly what I expected."

"Let me finish," Torberg said. "Purely by accident one of the guys here in the lab took that print and sent it in with another bunch of prints to FBI Quantico."

"And?"

"Turns out there's a federal fugitive warrant on your friend Sheila Mozkowski. Only they got her under the name Caroline McGill."

"No shit?" I said. "What's she wanted for?"

"Hijacking and grand theft. She and a couple of guys robbed a truck in San Pedro, California. November 28, 1979. She was the only one they got prints on."

"How'd they happen to have prints on her?"

"She was arrested a couple of times in the late sixties for shoplifting. And once in the mid-seventies for some kind of political thing."

"How much money did they get out of this hijacking?"

"One hundred seventy-two thousand dollars," Torberg said.

"Jesus, what was it—a Brink's truck?"

"As a matter of fact, yes. A university payroll—I forget which department."

I sat back on the chair, a little stunned. "This was genuine money. Not counterfeit?"

"Of course it was genuine. Brink's isn't in the business of transporting counterfeit money."

"Well, I'll be damned," I said.

I hung up on Torberg and dialed Luke Carson back.

"I've got some news for you," I told him. "A tech at CPD just told me that Sheila Mozkowski robbed a Brink's truck for one-hundred-and-seventy-plus grand back in '79. Coin of the realm. *And* she had two male sidekicks."

"You're thinking Adams and his accomplice?" Carson said.

"That's what I'm thinking."

"Do you have ID on the other guy?" he asked.

"No. Neither one of the men was ever ID'd, although it stands to reason that Adams was one of them."

"Yeah, it does. Only I don't understand something. If they ripped off the truck for real money, what happened to it? The stuff we took off of you was fake."

"I don't know," I told him. "Maybe Sheila hid the real geld in some secret spot, when she found out that Adams was back in town. Maybe she was setting him up for a con, the way she set him up for a bust in '88."

"You know it's funny you mention that bust," Carson said. "'Cause I checked with Cov PD when I was doing a background on Adams, and they said it wasn't a woman who gave them the tip."

"You're kidding."

"No, it was some guy who called the tip in—told 'em they could find a shitload of drugs on Bob Adams in room whatever. They went up there and caught Bob with a spike in his arm."

"You got me, then," I said, feeling at sea. "I'd assumed all along that Sheila had set him up."

"Maybe *she* had a partner, too," Carson said.

I could think of half a dozen of them in the stereo club alone. It got me wondering.

# 24

I DECIDED to pay Sherwood Loeffler a visit. As far as I knew he was the only member of the stereo club who hadn't slept with Sheila. And he was a gossip. I rang him up from the office and he told me to come out to his Fairfield home.

He was waiting on the front stoop when I drove up around eleven that Friday morning. In the days that had gone by I'd forgotten just how imposing Sherwood looked—with his loaded beard and his six-foot-eight-inch girth.

"Thought you crossed me off your list, Har'," he boomed as I walked up to his door. "Some little *faux pas* I made. Cain't imagine what."

He ushered me through the door into the sitting room.

"Kids are at school, wife's at work. Got nothing to do with myself. Care for a little Strauss?"

"What happened to Wagner?"

"I'm a little disgusted with him just at the moment."

I smiled. Sherwood went into the anteroom and a few moments later *Salome* came on his speakers.

"Old Richard the Third. Helluva composer."

"He was a Nazi, wasn't he?"

Sherwood sighed. "Christ, you sound like an Israeli season-ticket-holder. When you gonna understand that music and politics don't have nothing to do with each other."

"You really believe that?" I asked.

"No," Sherwood said. "But I don't want to fight about Strauss."

Salome began singing her first aria—to Jokanaan in the well where he'd been imprisoned by Herodias. It was seductive stuff, but it was a con job. I listened to it for a while before asking Sherwood what I'd come to ask him.

"You seen much of Leon?"

"Uh, no," Sherwood said. "He's been in my prayers though. Him and that poor fallen woman."

"Speaking of Sheila, your friend Peacock was . . ."

"Is *shtupping* the word you're look for?"

"Right. *Shtupping* Sheila back in '88, wasn't he?"

"Thereabouts, I reckon. Him and the French Foreign Legion." Sherwood eyed me cagily. "What'chu driving at, Harry?"

I told him about Bobby Adams and the Quality Court bust. Sherwood was quick when he wanted to be.

220

"So you think Sheila had her a partner back in '88?" he said.

"The thought has passed through my head."

"Well, let it pass on out your ear," he said, "'cause it wasn't Larry Peacock. That boy wouldn't sacrifice himself for the Queen of Sheba. He's commonsensical when it comes to women."

"A hundred and seventy grand makes a lot of sense."

"I'm telling you it ain't Larry. Now a foreigner like Pavel . . ."

I shook my head. "I don't think it was him."

"Well, let's see, then there's Philo."

"Calling the police?"

Sherwood nodded. "You got a point there."

We thought about it for a moment, while Salome sang to Jokanaan in the well.

"How 'bout Leon?" Sherwood said. "Jews are smart, ya know."

It wouldn't have occurred to anyone but Sherwood —at least not in that particular way. But once he'd said it, I had to admit Leon made sense—especially since he already knew about the one hundred and seventy grand that Adams was after. He'd been living with it in the freezer for thirteen years. It was a pretty comforting little nest egg, even for a music lover. Pavel Fleischer had wondered why Sheila hadn't told Leon about Bob Adams's record sale at the Quality Court—all those shaded dogs and Mercuries Leon so adored. Pavel had thought it was because Sheila was *shtupping* Bobby. But it could have been because neither she nor Leon wanted Adams to know that Leon existed.

"The solution has the virtue of simplicity," Sherwood said expansively, "as well as domesticity. Keeping it all in the family, so to speak."

"All right," I said, "let's say Leon did call the Covington cops and tip them off, after Sheila planted drugs in Bobby's room. Wouldn't Sheila have warned Leon about Adams when Adams got out of prison and looked her up two weeks ago? After all she'd been *shtupping* Adams for a week before he broke into the house, beat Leon up, and snatched her."

"Maybe she did warn him, Harry," Sherwood said, warming to the task of skewering his rival. "You think of that? Or maybe she was afraid Adams was gonna kill Leon, so she decided she was gonna pay Adams off on her own with that money she got from selling Leon's records."

And the counterfeit thirty grand, I said to myself. Sheila had talked movingly about paying Leon back for having saved her from a wayward life and bad company like Bobby-boy. Perhaps she *had* been trying to return the favor. Only her act of self-sacrifice had worked out very badly, as I pointed out to Sherman.

"If she was trying to protect him, then why did Leon end up getting beaten up and Sheila end up dead?"

Sherwood snickered sarcastically. "How'd Sheila know the crazy son-of-a-bitch was gonna go nuts, rob a drugstore, and kidnap her? And who says she's dead?"

"She's dead, Sherwood. The blood, the hair, the ax."

"The matchbook, them drugs, that ID, the second tip about Turfway. I been pondering it for some time.

And what I come up with is that it was all pretty damn convenient, from Sheila's point of view."

I didn't want to think about it.

"It'd be a mighty neat plan, wouldn't it?" he persisted. "Make it look like Adams killed her?"

"To get rid of him."

"And have all that money for herself."

It was neat all right. And I knew that Sheila had it in her to manipulate a stoned dumbbell like Adams into doing just about anything she wanted him to do—even after he'd kidnapped her. Like Pavel Fleischer had said, Sheila was good—best—at handling men. And she'd handled this one at least twice before, in '79 and '88. But I didn't buy it. Partly because it was Sherwood's theory and he was having too good a time making me squirm beneath it. Partly because it was too much like a goddamn detective story—too clever by half for a real-life crime. But mostly because of Leon Tubin. I just couldn't see him being involved in such a caper. Not with Sheila's life at stake.

"I suppose it was Sheila who phoned in the tip from Florence Mall?" I said.

"Sure it was. She's a performer—a trained singer. She could make her voice sound like a man's."

"Yeah? How'd she know when to make the call? How'd she'd know where the rendezvous was going to be? Leon and Adams decided on that."

"Too easy," Sherwood said with a disparaging look.

I could see that it had become a game to him—pin the tail on Leon.

"She either overheard Adams set the thing up or,

mebbe she told Leon in advance where and when to set the rendezvous when Adams called."

I started to ask him how the hell Leon could have known what Sheila had in mind without having had any contact with her except for the brief moment that Adams had allowed her to speak during the phone call to Jewish Hospital. I started to say it, then stopped.

A little orchestral bell rang—ding! Actually it was more like a cimbalon.

"He got that damn call from Caroline," I said out loud. "In the hospital on Sunday afternoon."

"Who's Caroline?" Sherwood asked.

"An alias that Sheila once used. Caroline McGill. The nurse said Leon had gotten a call from a Caroline on Sunday afternoon, *before* he got the call from Adams."

I started to feel a little sick to my stomach.

"Well, there you go," Sherwood said. "They set it up on the phone."

It would explain why Adams and I had ended up rendezvousing in a pea-soup fog. If the time and place of the rendezvous *had* been prearranged between Sheila and Leon they couldn't have predicted the bad weather at Latonia.

"Jesus, you're a devil!" I said to Loeffler.

Sherwood grinned. "Just playing his advocate. 'Sides I read this all in a book."

"What do you mean you read it in a book?" I said.

Sherwood chuckled. "I hate to tarnish my horned image, but I ain't being quite as original as you might think—or as devilish. All this speculation comes straight

224

out of a book I just read. My wife, Martha, brought it home with her from the library on Tuesday."

"What book?" I said with foreboding.

"It's by some woman from Nome. I forget her name. I think it's called *Well of Dreams.*"

"All that's in the book," I said, feeling my heart sink down to the bottom of the well.

"Yeah," Sherwood said. "Story's a little different. This woman's trying to get rid of her ex-husband, who's a mobster. That'd be your Adams part. She does most of the work herself but in the end she gets this dumb, loyal guy to help her out—that'd be Leon. A lot of the details are the same: the trail of clues in a motel room, a fake murder, a tip to the cops with the woman pretending to be a man. Only in the book she's a trained ventriloquist or something—not a singer. You should read the thing, Harry. Might pick up a few pointers." He gave me a concerned look. "Say, you look a little peaked."

I felt a little peaked.

"Does she get away with it?" I asked Loeffler.

"Yes she does, by God. She and this dumb, love-struck guy she comes to kinda like. They get away clean as a whistle."

I drove back to my office and called Al Foster at CPD.

"I need a LEADS sheet on Leon Tubin. You have his prints on file in Criminalistics. Ask Steve Torberg."

I described Leon to Al, then hung up and dialed LeRoy Anderson.

"Howdy, Harry," he said cheerfully. "What kin I do for ya?"

I said, "On Monday night when Adams called, did he set up the time for the ransom-exchange, or did Leon suggest Turfway at 6 A.M."

"Lemme think about it."

He thought about it while I stared at the wastebasket. *Well of Dreams* was still sitting inside it. I could see a corner of the jacket, looming like a shark fin in the sea of McDonald's wrappers and cardboard coffee cups.

"I believe Leon was the one who suggested it," LeRoy said. "'Cause I remember him writing down the word *Turfway* on the pad. And I only said what he wrote. You been out to see him this week?"

"I'm planning a visit real soon," I said between my teeth.

"Too late," LeRoy said.

I sat up in the chair.

"Wha'd'ya mean too late?"

"Why I jus' dropped him off at the airport this morning," LeRoy said cheerfully. "Me and the stereo club seen him off. He was so down in the mouth 'bout Sheila he decided to go off on a vacation."

"Where?"

"I think he went to California. Leastways that's where his family's from and where he went to school."

"In California?" I said dully.

"Correct-o," LeRoy said. "Family lives 'round 'bout San Pedro, I think he said."

"Of course he would."

"Huh? You sure you're O.K.? You sound weird."

"I'm fine, LeRoy. Just a little disappointed."

"Maybe you should take a vacation, too. A nice, long rest."

It's what I needed all right. A nice, long rest.

Pulling the office bottle out of the Mosler and a shot glass out of the desk, I poured myself a drink while I dialed Steve Torberg back at CPD Criminalistics. The radio was on in the background—a string trio, appropriately enough, tossing the melody among the three different voices.

"Yeah?" Torberg said after I'd said hello. "Was the info any help?"

"A regular lifesaver," I said, knocking back the first shot. "That, uh, Brink's robbery in San Pedro? You said there was a college payroll in the truck?"

I poured myself a second while he shuffled through some papers. "Yep. That's what it says here. I got the sheet right in front of me."

"You also said the cash was earmarked for a specific department at the college?"

"Lemme see." I took another sip of booze while he was off the line. "Yeah, here it is. It was the library department at UCLA. At the time they suspected an inside job, because whoever engineered it had information about the library payroll schedule. The timing of the robbery and the smoothness with which it was carried off were pretty impressive. There were some damn difficult angles to consider on this one—whoever did it had a well-organized mind."

"And thorough," I said, finishing the drink.

Leon Tubin was nothing if not thorough.

**25**

**I GOT THE REMAINDER** of the story piecemeal over the next few days. Maybe I should've read the book instead of waiting. Sheila Mozkowski obviously had.

By then the cops had lifted Sheila's prints off the matchbook and determined that the handwriting was hers, too. There were other little things she'd slipped up on: a bloody footprint on the walkway outside the Adams's family domicile—woman's shoe; the splash pattern of the blood on the basement floor—not from an ax wound; the hairs on the piece of tape that Philo had found at the Sleepy Bear—cut not yanked from Sheila's head. An expert sonographer iced the cake when he found that the voice on the second phone tip could be a woman's voice and not a man's. Something to do with fricatives and glottals and the pitch of the vowels.

As for Leon, it turned out that he had a record of

his own. Sort of. He was busted at a political rally at UCLA. The same rally Sheila had been busted at. I figured that's where they'd met. Young firebrands out to change the world. Their priorities had obviously changed by '79. I don't know how she'd talked a guy like Leon into robbing a Brink's armored car. But if anyone could do it Sheila could. Maybe she'd made it seem like some sort of political thing. Maybe she'd made it seem like a game and he'd just showed up at a real robbery. Date–grand theft.

Afterward Bobby D. had somehow gotten himself busted for heroin, and Sheila had taken the money and Leon in tow, settling down in quaint, conservative Cincinnati. Who'd ever look for them there? A low-profile, ex-hippie couple, just making ends meet. Leftovers from the refrigerator of life, with a little windfall in the refrigerator in the kitchen. Leon had his stereo. Sheila had her comeback dream and her lovers. And of course the freezer fund neither one of them could touch because it was still too hot.

A hundred and seventy grand in the fridge and she said they couldn't afford me. But it wasn't the cash outflow Sheila was afraid of. She didn't want that damn basement robbery looked into. She wanted Leon to go right on thinking it had been Sherwood Loeffler who had stolen his records, until she could take care of Bobby Detroit on her own. Why she hadn't let Leon in on what she was up to with Bobby—at least until after she got kidnapped—I didn't know. It could have been as simple as what Sherwood had suggested: she hadn't wanted Leon to get hurt. Which was, in fact, what happened when Adams caught up with the little man.

Maybe Adams was holding more than the theft of the money against Leon. Maybe Leon had also stolen his girl.

The Ludlow cops managed to pin down the flight Sheila and Leon had taken out of Cincinnati International on Friday morning. Even if the cops had had a head start, it would been hell trying to stop them. They'd boarded and reboarded and transferred so many times it took the UA computer a day to figure it all out. Part of the problem was the names they'd used. Caroline McGill and, get this, Robert Detroit. The Music Lovers reunion tour.

They'd landed somewhere in Europe on Saturday morning—Hamburg or London or Brussels or Rome. Even the computer couldn't figure that part out because they'd changed names again at a stopover in Greenland and apparently traded tickets with two other passengers. By the time they touched down in wherever, Sheila and Leon were whoever they wanted to be. And rich. A hundred and seventy thousand bucks rich. Money they couldn't have spent in the States—on comebacks and musical tours. A trip they couldn't afford to take until Bobby Detroit was behind bars for life.

I went to visit the original Bobby Detroit at St. Catherine's on Saturday afternoon. He was under guard, of course.

I sat down by the bed and stared for a minute at his battered face. Richard Wagner in chains. Despite the fact that he deserved the death penalty for killing the Bromley pharmacist I felt a little sorry for him. Not as sorry, however, as he felt for himself.

"I know what happened, Bobby," I said, sitting

down on a chair by the bed. "She fucked you again, didn't she?"

He stared straight ahead—at the far wall.

"I can understand why you beat Leon up so badly. I guess you'd been looking for him for about as long as you'd been looking for Sheila. At least you got to pay back that much.

"In case you're interested they took the hundred and seventy grand and went to Europe. They're having a great time on your dough. You could testify against them if you wanted to on the Brink's robbery. Maybe cut a deal on the druggist thing."

Slowly the man turned his enormous head my way. Richard Wagner looked at me for a long moment, then said, "Fuck it. When you're screwed, you're screwed. Let 'em have the bread."

But that wasn't the very end of it.

Several months later the police held an auction of Leon's belongings—his stereo and his records—which had been confiscated when they finally figured the scam out. My business had improved by then. Jo was back. I felt like a different, somewhat chastened detective. Anyway I decided to drive out to the auction—thinking I might run into Sherwood or Philo or LeRoy.

They were all there. Philo, Sherwood, LeRoy, Larry Peacock, Dave Barber, Pavel Fleischer, Hank Diamond. They fought over Leon's stereo remains like relatives cleaning out the old house. They got into a particularly vicious fight over a valuable shaded dog called *Witches' Brew*. Sherwood accused Philo of driving

up the prices and started calling him names. Philo
started calling Sherwood names. It was like old times.

I thought of Leon Tubin and that first evening in
my office. And that first night with Sheila on the couch.

Neither one of them had wanted anyone to get hurt
—not even Bob Adams. They just wanted him out of
their lives for good. Sheila had planned to do it with the
stolen records and the counterfeit thirty grand. And
when the junkie son-of-a-bitch had gone nuts and kidnapped her, she'd played it by ear—or by book. Leon
had ended up going along for the ride, probably the
same kind of ride he'd ended up taking back in '79.

It had cost him a lot. His records, his stereo, his
peaceful life among the music lovers. Plus the little man
had taken an awful beating for his true love. I'd believed
him when he said it was something he'd dreamed about
all his life, getting beat up for the girl he loved. Knowing Sheila, he was going to take a few more blows before
the money ran out and their whirlwind tour of Europe
was done.

After the auction was over—and tempers had
cooled—Sherwood invited us all back to this house for a
game called "Guess-'em." He'd play a piece on the
stereo, then everybody would have to guess who composed it.

The only one I got right was Wagner. But I had a
little extra incentive.

After the stereo session Sherwood walked me to the
front door. There was a pile of mail in his mail box. He
picked it up, thumbed through the letters, and gasped.

"What's wrong?" I asked him.

Paling, he handed me a postcard. It was a photograph of Bayreuth. On the back someone had written a message: "Having a wonderful time. Salzburg, Vienna, Bayreuth." There was no signature. There was none necessary. The postcard was postmarked "Berlin."

"That little son-of-a-bitch has all the luck," Sherwood fumed.

"Ah, you got his records, Sherwood."

"Yeah, but he got the world."

And so he had. Salzburg, Vienna, Bayreuth, Valhalla. The stuff that dreams are made of.